Several Devils

K. Simpson

The
Devil's
Workshop
Book 1

Mindancer Press Classic

Bedazzled Ink Publishing Company * Fairfield, California

978-1-934452-24-0 paperback

A Mindancer Press Classic

first published
May 2001
Justice House Publishing

republished
June 2004
Fortitude Press

Cover art
by
C. A. Casey

Mindancer Press
a division of
Bedazzled Ink Publishing Company
Fairfield, California
http://www.bedazzledink.com/mindancer

To Shaun Day, Maureen Sak, and Ian Rowan

Acknowledgments

Thanks to everyone who had anything to do with this story in any of its incarnations.

CHAPTER 1
LATE JULY, WEDNESDAY, 5 A.M.

Much too early the morning after the art director's party, the local station that I'd fallen asleep to went back on the air, shocking me as awake as I was ever going to get in this life.

"Good morning, Meridian, and welcome to 'Early Edition.' Daybreak Don will be along later with the latest forecast for your Wednesday. In our top story of the hour, police—"

I shifted uncomfortably on the couch. So *that* was where the remote was. Viciously, I pried the thing out of my spine and started punching buttons. No luck at that hour. Infomercial. Evangelism. Daybreak Don. Evangelism. Evangelism.

In no mood to be saved, sold, or slimed, I tried VH-1, which was just breaking for commercials. The first one—an orgy of models in Spandex, flouncing around to Van Halen—made me change channels as fast as I could. But I wasn't fast enough to miss the "spokesmodel" at the end. "Get it. Flaunt it," she was saying—unnecessarily, really, if you looked at her where the cameraman had.

Did it matter that nobody would know for sure that the commercial was for a health club? Did it matter that I'd written it?

Well, advertising was a living. Club West wasn't the worst work on my reel. And sex sells everything anyway. Why feel guilty about it?

I switched off the TV and crawled off the couch—a triumph

of will, under the circumstances—to start the coffeemaker and open the deck-door curtains.

The sky was red. Somehow, sky that color seemed right. So did the three crows, black as mortal sin, circling silently over the condos.

I squinted bloodshot up at them. Christ, they were big for crows. Maybe they were really ravens.

Ravens. Why not? The morning after that much wine, this far into thirtysomething, what you want is ravens. Poe knew all about these things. How did it go?

And his eyes have all the seeming of a demon's that is dreaming . . .

Now why did that line come to mind? Curious.

The ravens dipped and soared in the weird red sky, not making a sound. Watching them made me a little seasick, so I gave it up after a moment and went back to the kitchen to see whether the coffee was ready.

I drank one mug standing over the coffeemaker, poured another—and nearly dropped it on the way back to the great-room. A shadow was moving slowly across the carpet, the shadow of a woman, long hair blowing lightly in the hot wind.

Someone was out on the deck.

Keeping sharp watch on the shadow, I parked the mug on the counter, felt along the wall for the fireplace tools, and then edged toward the sliding glass door, gripping a poker, too scared to feel stupid. I took a deep breath, grabbed the door handle . . .

And swore, and threw the poker halfway across the room. *Now* I felt stupid. It was only one of the ravens, sitting on the deck rail, and the shadow that it cast was the shadow of a bird.

That did it—no more art directors' parties. Bad dreams all night, and now bad birds. I was starting to see things.

CS80

An hour or so later, I'd recovered enough to drive to work, thanks to caffeine. The shelf in the shower stall was just big enough to hold a travel mug, which was why I'd installed it. Some mornings, it had literally been a life-saver. I believed in coffee the way everyone else seemed to believe in God.

There *was* no God, of course, or any such thing as enough coffee, either. But you have to have faith in something.

Work? Not likely. I was in advertising, so my job was to lie—not that I had any real problem with that. I was good at lying, and well paid for it. But I had no illusions about my livelihood—therefore, no faith in it.

Community? Please. Mine was Meridian, a foursquare Midwestern city of nearly a million people but really just a big small town built on a Baptist rock. You couldn't find a more buttondown, plain-vanilla place outside Nick at Nite.

Actually, technically, nobody lived *in* Meridian anymore—at least, nobody I knew—but in the upscale burbs of the metroplex. The Beautiful People lived in Greenville, the most upscale and pretentious of them all. Of course, I lived there too. Except for the fact that I didn't have the cedar fence, the SUV, or the 2.3 Baby Gap brats, I might have passed, demographically, for anyone else on the better mailing lists.

All this was fine if you were born for it but worse than hell if you weren't. I wasn't sure whether I was or not. I'd been born in the area but had done too much time there and someday would have to get out. To a Real City, which had things like, say, real newspapers—as opposed to the *Meridian Herald,* which was printed entirely in crayon. I didn't have much use for the *Herald*—or for churches, or for the conventional white-picket-fence life. I wasn't married, engaged, dating anyone, or even just screwing around. Naturally, this made me evil.

And on top of all that, just look what I did for a living.

Still, I didn't think I was all *that* eccentric. It was true that I dressed funny, compared with most people—more or less like a veejay, mostly in black. It was also true that I would talk back to the Devil himself, if he happened to annoy me, which was too much attitude for most people. And then there was the celibacy. But you couldn't call me eccentric if you were a reasonable person. Take my best friend. She didn't think I was eccentric; she just thought I was crazy.

A little reputation for crazy didn't hurt in my line of work, though, and J/J/G Advertising was one of the few places in town where a person could get away with being different. Granted, not very —it *was* Meridian—but at least at J/J/G, people were used to me.

What I really believed in, I guessed—besides coffee— wasn't work or family or community or God, but the right to be a little different. No matter what anyone thought. Some people were sure that I was evil because I wasn't Just Like Everybody Else. OK—they had the right to be chicken-witted, hen-hearted morons that you couldn't tell apart *with* a scorecard. No matter what *I* thought. Difference again.

I wished that my small departures from convention made me happier, though. The trouble, I was starting to think, was that I couldn't decide what was scarier: being the same, or being different.

Maybe that was why I'd been having the bad dreams lately. Those dreams could be why the shadow had scared me. It could have been my Shadow, come to haunt me outside my head while I was awake and ready to recognize it for—

Naaah. That would be crazy. Besides, Jung was too much work at that hour.

All that thinking was making my head hurt again, so I cranked up David Byrne on the MG's tape deck.

Glancing into the rear-view mirror before changing lanes for the 10th Street exit, I would have sworn—for a second—

that someone was in the back of the MG, in the well behind the seats.

Unnerved, I jerked around to check. Nothing.

"Crazy," I told myself firmly, and cut off a jacked-up Chevy pickup with a shotgun hanging in the back window.

⋘⋙

"Morning, Devvy. You look lifelike today."

Not amused, I turned from the coffeemaker to the source of the commentary. Cassie, damn her. *She* looked like something out of *Vogue*, as usual—every long, naturally blonde hair in place; both eyes clear, blue, and alert. How? The woman was three months older than me. And just hours ago, she'd been so crazed on cheap tequila that she'd offered to have Randy Harris' baby, right there in the art director's living room. Randy Harris, for God's sake. Cass was so out of her box last night.

Yet there she stood, the hypocrite, all business, far above her past. She was lucky she had a client with her; otherwise, I'd have had words.

"This," she told the client, "is Devlin Kerry. One of our assistant creative directors. Actually, she's our assistant creative director in charge of sex. You've seen the Club West series?"

The client gaped. "Club West?"

"That's our Devvy. Or *was*. You'll have to excuse her this morning. There was a little party last night, and . . . well, you see."

Over the back of the client's head, I narrowed my eyes at her.

"Club West," the client repeated. Then he turned to me. "Yes. I know those commercials. Maybe you could do one like that for us."

Over the back of the client's head, Cassie shot me a Meaningful Look.

"I don't see why not," I said, raising my mug. "What's your product?"

"Service, Miss Kerry. Service. Mortuary service."

I spat coffee halfway across the staff kitchen. Cassie's expression went from meaningful to murderous.

"Well, we *do* have an image problem," the client said, injured.

"There are no problems, Mr. Kester. Only challenges. And we're here to help you meet them." Cassie gave him her very sweetest smile. It worked. It always worked. "Why don't we go upstairs and see Mr. Jenner now?"

As she herded the client past, she stuck a sharp elbow in my ribs. Right—I'd missed my cue again.

"Pleasure," I lied, extending a hand. The client shook it gingerly.

As soon as they were gone, of course, I wiped off the hand he'd shaken. You can't be too careful with clients.

Or, in this business, with co-workers. And especially not with Cassie. I knew where *she'd* been.

ॐ

The day went straight downhill from there. Most of the other party survivors stopped by to tell me how *well* they felt. An illustrator quit, at the top of his lungs, all over the third floor, for nearly an hour. Two copywriters who couldn't agree on whether "mondo" was a word stabbed each other with pencils. And the word from the fourth floor was that Jenner, the head case who owned the agency, had punched out the head of the agency's law firm again, for whatever reason this time. I blamed the weird, violent mood of the day on the weather— solid rolling thunderstorms—and on Cassie's bad karma for bringing a mortician into the building.

Late in the afternoon, the Karma Queen herself dropped by,

still mad, to give me what for. I was more than ready to give it right back.

"You venial bitch," I said. "You yuppie-scum bloodsucker. You evil greedy sow. All this *oinking* over a commission you lost. It's not my fault. I'm not responsible for your misadventures. Anyone with detectable IQ would know not to pitch sex to an undertaker, dammit. You must be out of your tiny mind. You must be—"

"You twisted creep. You two-bit pornographer. You make Caligula look like a piker. You are just too perverted for words. But let me see if I can find a few. Starting with—"

"Philistine."

"Caligula's horse. Caligula's horse's *ass*."

"I never liked you."

"I never liked you first. I hated you the minute I met you, just to start getting in practice. You are *the* worst, *the* most terrible, *the*—"

I checked my watch. "Right. That's five. Are we through?"

"We're through. Thanks." Breathing relief, she sank back into my guest chair. "So why don't I buy you a drink? Or are you too good to drink with an account manager?"

"Depends on the account manager."

"Come on. I'm buying. We'll celebrate the Kester Mortuaries account."

Jolted, I sat up all the way. "What?"

"I got the account."

"You got the account? You mean you just put me through a Five Minutes' Hate over an account you already *had*?"

"Get over it, Devvy. I needed to fight with somebody today. You have no idea what a hangover I've got."

"Don't tell me your troubles. *My* head feels like a chemistry experiment."

"Whose fault is that? I tried to warn you about the wine. *If* that's what it was. Greg said he thought he saw a tanker truck pull up to the back door around ten." She rubbed her temples, wincing. "Do you know you gave another State of the Union last night?"

Really? I vaguely remembered climbing up on the bar at one point, but mercifully, memory failed after that.

Cassie, not merciful and possessed of excellent memory, filled in the blanks.

"—and then you said that because you burn off *your* sex drive by working out—at Club West, for the love of God!—you were going to swim the English Channel this weekend. In an hour, coast to coast. Then you told Randy Harris he was a mortally stupid prick and if he didn't stop laughing, you'd take his balls along as shark bait, if he *had* any. *Then* you said—"

"All right, dammit, so I got a little personal."

"You got a *lot* personal. But you were right about the 'stupid' part. Did you know he asked me to have his baby? Right there behind the loveseat?"

I smiled wolfishly. "Convenient memory, Cass. The way *I* remember it—"

"You remember nothing; you were crocked. And so was he. I *hope*."

Thoughtful silence descended on us. In that silence, we heard thunder rumbling again. I glanced out the window and then back at Cassie, who was staring at me. "What?"

"I worry about you sometimes. I really do. I think this celibacy business is making you weird. Weird*er*. Celibacy's fine for nuns and monks and nine-year-olds, but you don't have any religion, and you're getting older every birthday. How long's it been now? Four years?"

"Six."

"*Six?* Devvy, that's obscene. You have *got* to let me help you. I'm your best friend. You can trust me. I'll fix you up with a reasonably decent guy. Always assuming that there *is* one.

But you leave that to me." Inspired now, Cassie got up. "Come on—we'll go to the Pig & Whistle. I met a cute stockbroker there a couple of weeks ago."

"Just what I need in this whole wide world. A stockbroker." Tolerance exhausted, I crossed my arms and glared at her. "Some friend you are. A stockbroker? My *landlord's* a stock—"

"You big hypocrite. You make all these sweaty sex-on-the-beach ads, and you don't even *have* sex anymore. Where do you get this stuff?"

"Sublimation, baby duck. It's all in the sublimation."

Cassie shook her head. "You're going to blow like Vesuvius one of these days. You're not safe to be around. Are you coming with me?"

"Sorry."

"You'll *be* sorry. When you're dead and in Hell, you'll wish you had those six years back."

"We'll talk about it in Hell, then. If *I'm* going, I know for a fact that *you're* going. They'll probably roast us on the same pitchfork, with my luck." Ostentatiously, I checked my watch again. "I've got work to do. Go without me. So long."

There was a long silence with no footsteps in it. I looked up. She was still there, and she was staring again.

"*What?*"

"I wish I understood you better, Devvy."

"Don't get sentimental on me now. We've known each other too long. Go. *Go* to the Pig & Whistle. Don't forget to stop by the drugstore on the way. See you tomorrow."

Cassie left, muttering, and banged the door open on her way out.

At which point I switched off the desk lamp and turned to brood out the window for a while.

◈

Cassie *was* my best friend, and she *did* understand me well enough. As soon as she met me, she'd said once, she knew I had a big bad attitude and a big bad bark and no bite at all, and so, she'd said, we were going to get along perfectly, because *she* had the bite. She was right. She was too smart to sell advertising but liked the money too much not to. She also liked the thrill of the chase. And she liked me, so far as I knew, because I was always good for a verbal workout. Everyone else seemed to figure that because she was beautiful, she was fragile and about as bright as a firefly.

She *was* beautiful, all right, not that I cared what she looked like, although if I'd had to describe her, I would have said that she had the face of a troublemaking angel. She said I looked like my own evil twin, so you see why I qualify the "angel" part. Men fell like dominoes at her feet, and Cassie adored dominoes. That probably was another reason why she liked me: I wasn't competition. She had trouble keeping female friends, and I figured that she was grateful for one ally among her kind. Even if that ally was me.

Why I wasn't competition was what she didn't understand. In truth, neither did I. Celibacy was just the best solution I could find for a solutionless problem.

It wasn't that I didn't have good reason: It wasn't worth risking HIV for something that had never been any good anyway. In my experience, sex was overrated, to say the absolute least. I still felt that way. So did many of the women I knew. "Men," they'd say, resigned, disgusted. "Go figure."

Well, I *had* tried to figure. I had tried, period. But it was no use. Six years ago, I'd finally decided that men simply didn't work for me. I didn't hate them. I didn't want them exterminated. I just didn't want to date them anymore.

But I wasn't interested in the alternative, either. Wasn't my style. And it was probably too late to cross that street anyway.

Not that I hadn't wondered about it from time to time. Given my work, I was forced to deal with models, some of whom were stunning, some of whom were friendlier with me than absolutely necessary, and I'd sometimes wondered whether everything I'd heard about models was true. Still, I had a vague idea of what a Ms. Right might be, and she wouldn't be some jailbaity airhead. She'd probably be a grown woman with all kinds of IQ, with a certain sense of humor—and OK, dammit, with movie-star looks. And it would be best for her to be wildly inappropriate and utterly inaccessible. Safest that way, you see.

But even more inappropriate and inaccessible, and much less safe, was the woman I'd been dreaming about for the past six weeks or so.

Dreams were nothing new. Neither were nightmares, really. But these nightmares were different—so real that I would swear I was awake.

I figured some old Dracula movie was making trouble in my subconscious, for some reason. The nightmares were always the same, and close enough to the films to fit that theory: my room would fill up with fog, and then there would be a vampire in my bed. The fact that this vampire was a she, not a he, was a minor detail as far as I could tell; a bite in the neck is a bite in the neck.

And the fact that the dreams, perversely, got a little sexual was a fact that I didn't care to examine. Movies are *supposed* to turn people on. It wasn't my fault.

Somehow, though, I knew that this explanation was only smoke. Whatever was down there in the dark of those dreams wasn't coming from any movie. I could almost swear that I was really feeling a draft from an open window and really seeing moonlight on a sweep of long black hair. The dream was always the same, down to the needle-point pressure of the fangs at my throat and then the pause before—

"Dev?"

I jumped several feet straight up. Kurt whistled softly.

"Jesus, boss. How much coffee today?"

"Never do that again. *Ever*. What do you want?"

"Nothing. I was leaving, and I saw your door was open. What are you doing sitting in the dark?"

When had it gotten dark? "I was meditating."

"Uh-huh." He sounded unconvinced, which was just as well. J/J/G, like all agencies, already had enough dumb copywriters, and he already looked too much like a Stooge for my comfort. Larry, maybe, if Larry had had a walrus mustache. "I saw Cassie a couple of hours ago. She said you two were going out to pick up sailors. I had to remind her that Meridian is landlocked. What happened?"

"I wasn't in the mood."

Kurt grinned and settled familiarly on the edge of my desk. "That's the trouble with you, boss. You never are."

"And the trouble with her," I countered, "is that she never isn't."

"I don't know about that. She's just a little *too* convincing sometimes. Know what I mean?"

No. But I knew he was going to tell me. The trouble with Kurt was that he'd never gotten over Psych 101. He'd minored in Human Behavior and now spent too much of his time analyzing ours. Heather, his copywriting partner, came to my office at least once a week to ask whether I cared if she killed him.

"The thing with Cass is that she protests too much," he said. "Nobody's *that* straight. In fact, nobody *is* straight—not all the way. You've heard of the Kinsey Scale? Zero all straight, six all gay?"

I reached for my coffee, which was stone-cold by then, and took a long swallow. "So?"

"So she's probably sexually confused. Not sure where she

really falls on the scale. So she's acting out. You probably are, too. This celibacy stuff isn't natural any more than female promiscuity is. Are there feelings you're not in touch with? Is there something you're repressing?"

"The only thing I'm repressing right *now*, son, is my desire to make you dead. Sex is my livelihood, not my life. And it's none of your business anyway. Now you should get out of my office, while you still can."

Kurt laughed. "This would cost you a hundred bucks an hour anywhere else. You're getting it free. Want me to tell you about your childhood?"

"We may be overstaffed with copywriters," I said darkly. "I may need to fire you. Let me sleep on it, and I'll get back to you. In the meantime, tell me this: Where do *you* fall on the scale?"

"Zero. A perfect zero. I'm the exception that proves the rule."

"Fine. You're fired now."

"Too bad you don't have a sense of humor, boss."

"Tell me something funny and we'll see. Tell me about *your* sex life. What's the zero for, besides the obvious? And does your wife know?"

"Biblically?"

I ignored that. "Maybe *you* protest too much. If all humans are bisexual at heart, and if you're human—and we won't know for sure till the autopsy—just how bi are you?"

"Me? Bi? Don't talk crazy." He winked and eased off my desk. "Well, good night. You ought to head home yourself. They've got tornado warnings out. We could all be in Oz tonight."

"Fine. Walk me to my car. I've had enough Oz for one day."

☙❧

The elevator took what seemed to be an unusually long time to come. When the doors finally opened, I walked in, lost in thought about Kurt's damn scale—and almost walked into the most gorgeous woman in the world. Forget the movies, forget the magazine covers. This was a whole different order of gorgeous.

And there was no question that she was the woman in my dreams.

Struck dumb, I simply stared at her. She stared back, all the way through me, her black hair and black gown blowing in a nonexistent wind. Her eyes were the color of rubies, with peculiar lights. I'd never seen eyes quite that color before.

Slowly, she smiled—and to my horror, two razor-sharp fangs began to rise in the perfect red curve of her mouth.

"Dev? What's the matter?"

The instant Kurt spoke, the woman vanished. Disbelieving, I passed my hand through the clear air where she'd been standing.

"Did you see that?" I asked.

"See what?"

"Her."

"Her who?"

When I didn't answer, he gave me a long clinical look. Then he tapped the big print on the back of the elevator car. "Bouncing Betsy. We've used her at least a dozen times. This is *yours*."

So it was—the first print piece of the new Club West campaign. I hadn't even noticed it till then. But he didn't have to know that.

"It scared me," I said lamely.

"*They* scared you, you mean. That's OK. They even scare me. Do you suppose she goes out with married men?"

Rather harder than necessary, I pushed the lobby button.

CHAPTER 2

THURSDAY

Kurt and Heather were a little late for the team meeting the next morning, but never mind—I was there only in body myself, having had the nightmare all night. Besides, the creative director was in charge of the meeting, which was only about the Rumours account.

The account was Chip's fault. I liked Chip, even though he was an account exec and even though he looked like a country-club version of Aryan Youth, but I had grave doubts about his client list. He had a bad habit of taking dares, which was why we were stuck with this new client of his: a disco-trash nightclub with an interesting reputation.

I didn't like clients with interesting reputations, especially not at that hour of the morning. So I lasered the guilty party over the rim of my coffee mug while the creative director called the meeting to order, after a fashion.

"—look forward to these meetings all week," Jack was saying, "because you people are so perverse. I often wonder what you do when you're alone."

"Shhhh," Heather told him, mock-horrified. "If you make us tell, Dev'll make us put it in an ad."

I lasered her, too.

Jack laughed. "Looks like Kerry's in a mood. The Danger is rising. We'll just have to work around her. What've we got today?"

"Rumours," Kurt said.

"Rumours." Jack shook his head. "God. You'd better be as good as you think you are. Who wants to start?"

Kurt did. What else was new? He gave us a good five minutes on some lame Village People concept, heavy on the concept. Heather rolled her eyes. Troy, our art director, drew a mushroom cloud on his notepad.

"No," Jack said. "Next?"

Heather tried her luck with something else out of retro hell. Troy drew a dripping knife. Kurt made artillery noises.

"Jesus. You slackers wouldn't think the '70s were so damn cute if you'd *been* there." Jack leaned back in his chair and winked at me—a try at generational bonding, I supposed, but I was having none of it. "Up to you now, Kerry. What've you got? Anything?"

I told him I'd get back to him.

"Nothing? Not even another bad idea?"

"Give me a day or two, Jack. I've been wrapping up the radio for Club West all week."

He cocked an eyebrow. "Sex is sex. What's the difference between that client and this one? Just that Club West leaves the lights on. You *can't* be blocked on this one. What's the problem?"

"Celibacy," Kurt suggested.

Most days, I would've taken the bait with pleasure— another chance to do a State of the Union. That day, though, I wasn't sure he wasn't right. So I said nothing.

"The assistant creative director in charge of sex," Jack intoned, "is blocked. Heaven help us. She listens to leather and polyester, and she can't even come up with feathers. What do you suppose—"

"Quit trying to yank my chain," I told him. "I don't have Kurt's *range*. Homoerotic fantasies are a little out of my line."

"For Rumours, they probably ought to be the *whole* line.

The client's got the rep. We don't have to like it; we just have to make money on it. Who wants to try to reeducate Kerry about diversity?"

I told him that Political Correctness was, in my opinion, a crime against reason. I was about to add that his hair plugs were, too, when Troy broke in.

"What if we put Connie the Barbarian on the case?"

"Not even as a joke," I warned.

No kidding. Connie the Barbarian, who did something or other in the mailroom, made the Chicago Bears' defensive line look sissy. She was a big, mean-looking stereotype on the hoof, and she made all the women at J/J/G very, very nervous. Most of the men, too, for that matter. Down the table, Chip shuddered.

Jack smirked at me, pleased with himself for having gotten something started. "You can't see past the beast to the inner beauty?"

"Beauty, as in a really cute warthog?"

Titters. "She's deep," Heather said.

"She's right," Jack told me. "That's what I've always liked about you, Kerry, you're deep. You're very deep—on the surface. In fact, I daresay you're *all* surface."

I regarded him in smoldering silence, wondering where I could bury the body.

"Of course," he added, "I mean that as a compliment."

Everyone waited for me to shoot back. For spite, I didn't. Jack thought for a second and then tried a different tack. "Maybe this celibacy thing with her is religious. Maybe the Baptists finally got to her. But maybe we can still save her. *After* we figure out the Rumours campaign, of course. What about this, Kerry: dancing transvestites in garter belts and sensible shoes?"

That did it.

"There are limits to everyone's Correctness," I snapped,

"and you just hit *my* limit, mister. If you want to play to the cheap seats, fine. But some of my best friends—"

Groans went up around the room. Hating myself for having stepped in that one, I made very sure not to look at Troy.

That slip was Kurt's fault. He insisted that Troy was gay because Troy wore a tie to work most days—but then, Kurt didn't own a tie that didn't have cartoon characters on it, so what did he know? Still, he'd planted the bad seed in my mind, and apparently, it had put down roots.

How stupid was I that I'd actually listened to Kurt? I *liked* Troy. I couldn't care less who he slept with, even if it was with another guy—which it probably wasn't, because I'd caught him once making out in a stairwell with a girl from Marketing, but it didn't matter if it was. Furthermore, I really *did* have gay friends. Not many, because not many men in Meridian were openly gay, but I got on like a house on fire with art directors and illustrators and photographers and—

Stupid. Stupid. God, had I ever met a stereotype I didn't like?

"Never mind," I told Jack. "Never *mind*. I don't care what people do in their private lives, just as long as they don't make me *look*. But that's just what I'm trying to say about your harebrained idea. Your *latest* harebrained idea, I mean. I don't see any reason to alienate ninety percent of the market just to—"

"Ninety-seven percent. New study."

"—just to make people look at an ad. Shut up, Kurt."

"We may be on to something here," Jack mused. "Why settle for ninety-seven percent when you can have the whole market? Why not offend everybody, while we're at it? Remember *Blazing Saddles*?"

It is impossible to overstate the danger of mentioning certain movies around advertising types, most of whom aren't wrapped too tightly to start with. In seconds, everybody else in the room was doing scenes from the movie. Verbatim. In character. Loud.

The meeting was over at that point, so I left. Halfway down the hall, I realized that I'd had a splitting headache for a while . . . and decided to blame Chip for that, too.

෬෨

When I left the office that night, my head still hurt, probably from fighting writer's block all day. Jack was right. I couldn't be blocked on this one. So what *was* the problem?

Burnout, maybe, or the slow return of sanity. If my own ads were starting to make me uncomfortable, maybe it was time to throttle back.

Besides, I'd never asked to be assistant creative director in charge of sex, or anything else. I'd been perfectly happy as a copywriter. But then, a few months ago, I'd had to write "Genesis."

CLIENT: Village Florists
TITLE: "Genesis" (30 seconds)
MUSIC: Vivaldi's "Four Seasons," Spring movement
SCENE 1 (6 sec.): Exterior; morning; a garden being planted. A woman's hand in the foreground, holding a rose plant. The hand fondles the root—slowly, in extreme closeup.
SCENE 2 (6 sec.): Exterior, day: same garden as Scene 1, but with roses starting to bloom. A man's hand appears. The index finger probes a half-opened rose, trying to open it.
SCENE 3 (6 sec.): Interior, afternoon; a kitchen. A woman's hand places three or four roses in a crystal vase. A man's hand appears, holding a watering can. The hand pours water into the vase. Too much water—the vase overflows.

SCENE 4 (12 sec.): Interior, night; a bedroom. An unmade bed; half-full wineglasses on the night table; man's and woman's shoes next to the bed. Slowly pan in on the rose petals scattered in the sheets.
TITLE (Scene 4 after 6 sec.), above VILLAGE FLORISTS logo: IT'S NOT TOO LATE TO START SOMETHING TONIGHT.

I hadn't wanted the project. What did I know about this stuff? But Jack insisted, probably because he knew that it would irritate me, so for payback, I wrote the most vulgar script I could devise. It took all of ten minutes.

How was I to know that the damn thing would take off the way it did? The local TV stations got so many complaints from the Family Foundation and church groups that we had to pull the spot off broadcast TV. But it was very popular on late-night cable. As a result, the agency started to attract attention—and, more important, clients.

Jenner ordered me to keep it up. It was my curse to turn out to have some knack for this sort of thing, so I had no choice, and after I finished my first campaign for Club West, he promoted me. I'd been stuck in management ever since, Peter Principled within an inch of my life. I suspected that Cassie had something to do with the promotion—Jack, I knew, had opposed it—but could never prove it. Besides, it was too late now.

Even worse than the promotion, though, was the rep that had come with it. At a party not long after "Genesis" went on the air, Jack and a video editor got several drinks for the better and started to speculate about my sex life. Not being stone—cold sober myself, I told them that I was celibate and what they should go off and do to themselves. The word was all over J/J/G the following Monday. Thereafter, hardly a day went by that some twerp didn't bother me about celibacy.

Lately, the bothering seemed to be happening more and more often. At the same time, having to think about sex so much at work was starting to carry over into my thinking at home. Which may have been why I'd been drinking a little too much. And/or why I was having the dreams.

Who knew, though? Besides, work was the real problem. I was blocked—couldn't come anywhere near a target that I should've been able to bull's-eye in my sleep. That wasn't good. But . . .

Oh, hell, what difference did it make? It wasn't art. It was only advertising.

I decided to drop it all and worry again in the morning. Meanwhile, I'd go home, soak in a hot bath, have a brandy or two, and then sleep. Dreamlessly, if possible. In the morning, I'd call Dr. Shapiro. *I'm nervous, Doc. What have you got for nervous?*

Xanax, maybe. I could ask her for Xanax. And animal tranquilizers for Kurt.

Kurt. *There* was a specimen. I wondered what Cracker Jack box his wife had found him in. A writer that obnoxious would probably make a first-rate serial killer—or creative director— someday.

Come to think of it, though, people said the creative-director thing about me, too. Now, that *really* wasn't good.

For relief from the noise of my thoughts, I stuck a Go-Go's cassette in the car's tape deck. I loved the Go-Go's. Sometimes I liked to infuriate Cassie by telling her that "Skidmarks on My Heart" was the greatest pop song ever written.

I fast-forwarded to "Skidmarks" and put the little MG in high gear. That was the closest to happy I'd been all day.

But nothing lasts. A couple of blocks from the office, I glanced into the rear-view mirror—and saw a pair of glittering red eyes right over my shoulder.

I promptly lost control of the car, which swerved on the

wet street and went spinning through the intersection. The next thing I knew, the MG was upside down in the hedges outside an office building.

And dammit, my Go-Go's tape was ruined, too.

CHAPTER 3
FRIDAY

First thing in the morning, I called the doctor, Jack's answering service, and a taxi, in that order. Then I left a message on Cassie's voice mail. Seven in the morning, and she wasn't home. Must've had luck—or something—last night.

I was in Dr. Shapiro's office at eight-thirty and home half an hour later, loaded down with samples of some antianxiety drug that Shapiro thought might help in a week or so. She didn't trust me with Xanax, she'd said, adding that if I'd been seeing things, the best medicine she could prescribe anyway was rest.

Precisely *what* things I'd been seeing, I hadn't told her. By daylight, the story seemed ridiculous, and who would believe it if I didn't?

Scroogelike, I chalked everything up to physical causes. I'd probably gotten hold of poisoned wine at that party and bad brandy at home. On top of that, I'd been working too many hours lately. Stress and poisonings might be just enough to make anyone check out of reality. Shapiro was no fun, but she was probably right.

So I turned up the air conditioning and went back to bed. When I finally got up, it was only to order a pizza and camp out on the greatroom couch downstairs, which was where I still was, watching a movie, when Cassie and Chip walked in. I'd ignored the doorbell, but Cassie knew where I hid the spare key.

"So you *are* alive," Chip said, in lieu of hello. "She said you would be. She said you're too evil to die. Going in for stunt driving these days, are you?"

"Go away," I said.

He just smiled. "You might want to take some classes, though, if you're serious about it. Sounds like you're not very *good* at it yet."

Cassie scowled at him and then threw the spare key in the general direction of the couch. "You have the nerve of the world, Devvy, leaving me that message and then not answering your phone all day. Why didn't you pick up?"

"Phone didn't ring. I turned the ringer off. Want some pizza?"

She studied the leftovers with suspicion. Then she surveyed the couch and the coffee table. An empty carton of Ben & Jerry's, with the spoon still in it. An ashtray full of M&Ms. A half-bag of caramel popcorn. Part of a jar of artificial cheese. A few empty frappucino bottles. Et cetera. Et cetera. Her eyebrows arched.

"It's not that bad, Cass," Chip assured her. "You never lived in a frat house. You haven't *seen* squalor." His expression grew thoughtful. "I'd have to say this is pretty darn close, though. What's on the lip of that bottle, Dev? Pizza sauce?"

Cassie's jaw dropped. "Do you mean to tell me that you've been drinking Coke right out of a two-liter bottle?"

I had been, as it happened, and did again then, just to annoy her. Chip laughed, though, and reached for the M&Ms.

"Have some popcorn, too," I urged. "It's the caramel kind. Try it with Cheez Whiz."

Cassie said a very bad word and left the room.

"Are you sure you weren't one of my frat brothers?" Chip asked. "Maybe the one who didn't wash his sheets for a whole semester?"

"I don't *live* like this, son. This is just for the duration of my breakdown. What are you two doing here?"

"Client meeting at three. She wanted to stop by and check on you. You're sort of on the way." He fished some popcorn out of the bag and looked at me questioningly. I nodded. Carefully, so as not to get anything on his nice linen suit, he dunked the popcorn in the Cheez Whiz. "So really, how are you? There's a rumor going around the office that you totaled your car and you're in a coma."

"I *am* in a coma. Move. I can't see the TV."

Cassie came back from wherever she'd been in time to hear that. "You've seen that movie a hundred times. You've made *me* see it a hundred times." To Chip, she added, "She knows all the dialogue. You have no idea how annoying—"

Happy to demonstrate, I did. Not amused, Cassie stepped between me and the screen.

"We're leaving," she declared. "This place is unspeakable. I can't imagine what's gotten into you. Are you going to the party tonight?"

"What party?" I asked.

"Greg and Linda's. I know you know."

"Oh. *That* party. I don't know. Wouldn't it be bad form to stay home from work and then show up at a party?"

"Bad form never stopped *you* from anything before," Cassie said exquisitely. "Is your car still in the shop?"

"Yup."

"All right, then, Mark and I'll stop by to pick you up at seven."

"How bad is it?" Chip asked, all interest. He drove a restored Triumph himself.

"Not very," I said. "A few dings. They're putting a new top on. I'm supposed to get it back tomorrow afternoon."

"How much are they charging you this time?"

I started to point out the futility of trying to predict a car-repair bill, but Cassie interrupted. "The party, Devvy. Seven. Sharp. Got that?"

"I'm not going on your date with you, lady," I told her. "It would look pathetic."

"It'll *be* pathetic. We'll pick you up at seven. Come on, Chip. *Some* of us work."

I threw an M&M—a red one, the lucky kind—after her. I was feeling better already.

⊂⊃

The party was well off the ground by the time Cassie, Mark, and I got there, and I lost no time in losing them—to Cassie's relief, I knew. This was her third date with him, which meant he knew how to listen, and Cassie liked that in a man. She already had that let's-find-a-coat-closet look in her eye.

For my part, I decided to find the bar. Greg had the Dead on the surround-sound system, loud, and odds were that it would be a long, long evening.

⊂⊃

Along about eight, I slipped out the back door to hide in the garden. Linda, like so many people nowadays, was a militant ex-smoker, and even though I'd finally quit myself the year before, I made her nervous. Every time I came to the house, she followed me around with a box of nicotine gum, talking loudly about the danger of relapse at parties. As though I were trailer trash who might light up in her cute pink bathrooms.

Outside would have been a better place to smoke anyway, though, on such a beautiful night. Unseasonably cool, since those storms the other day, but practically perfect—brilliant full moon, an ocean of stars, and down where I was, the sweet green fragrance of growing things. Something else, too—some sort of perfume, maybe; something exotic. Maybe Linda had hounded some other ex-smoker out of the house. Or maybe I was just imagining things. Nobody was around.

Wandering around the garden, I came upon a stocked pond. Koi, of course—the yuppie goldfish. Still, they were pretty, shimmering in the moonlit water like lamé, and watching them was oddly hypnotic.

Vaguely, I remembered hearing that watching fish can lower a person's blood pressure. I *had* been under a lot of stress. The better to lower my blood pressure, I leaned farther forward, to look deeper into the pond . . .

. . . and almost went in. Reflected in the calm water was the woman who'd been haunting me.

"Stop it, dammit!" I shouted at the image. "You know you're not real!"

Immediately, I felt a real, corporeal hand light on my shoulder. When I spun around, the real, corporeal woman was standing there.

She studied my face for a moment, and then threw back her dark head and laughed. Smokily, sexily, knowingly.

All my physical machinery ground to a stop. I *knew* that laughter. It was as intimately familiar as my heartbeat.

As familiar, in fact, as her touch had been. Impossible.

"A beautiful night for a haunting." Her voice matched her looks—and I knew the voice, too, somehow. "Cigarette?"

Wordless, I shook my head. She reached into the bodice of her black gown and produced a lighted cigarette—quite a trick for a ghost. Then she drew on it, inhaled deeply, exhaled slowly, almost theatri—

Wait a minute—ghosts didn't smoke.

Did they?

"I'm not a ghost. I'm a demon. *Your* demon." Her red mouth curved into a mocking little smile. "Your guardian devil, if you like. I thought you'd appreciate my wit in coming for you in a garden."

"How did you—?"

"Hell is practically all gardens. You never hear about gardens in heaven, do you? That damned Adam-and-Eve story. Have a cigarette, Devlin. You look as though you want one."

True enough. I'd never stopped wanting one. The patches had helped, but they cost a fortune. Otherwise, I'd have worn them for the rest of my life. On my worst days, I'd even contemplated smoking them.

Perhaps reading my mind, the woman pulled another lighted cigarette out of her bodice. How did she *do* that?

"No, thanks," I told her. "Really. I quit."

She put both cigarettes, still lighted, back where she got them from in the first place. Alarmed, I turned toward the koi pond. We'd need water when she started to burn.

But she didn't burn. She just smiled. "Go on. Take a good look. Take your time."

I felt a little criminal about it, but I did. Besides, that dress almost demanded attention. It looked like something Morticia Addams would wear to a funeral. The black silk was as snug as a racing glove all the way to the ground and cut much lower than functionally necessary. I wondered how she got into it, much less got around in it. I also wondered why she was wearing a crucifix. It appeared to be decorated with rubies, which went well with those eyes of hers, but it was still a crucifix—and parked way too low, at that. What was wrong with this picture?

"So you're my demon," I finally said. "You'll notice that I'm not arguing with you—I've been drinking. Do you have a name?"

"Would it amuse you if I said, 'We are Legion'?"

I scowled at her. She was too literate to be a devil.

"I heard that," she said. "I'm not a devil. I'm a demon. And *you're* too literate to be in advertising. But then, you're really in it for the sublimation, aren't you?"

She knew too much. But what worried me even more was the chance that she might know everything.

"Monica," she said suddenly. "My name is Monica. And I *do* know everything about you. Shall I prove it?"

"No. You're a nightmare. I'll wake up when you bite."

She threw back her head and laughed again. Again, that terrible, inexplicable familiarity tugged at me.

"Walk with me," Monica said.

ও৪৪৩

We never went back to the party. We wound up at a coffee-house on Shipley Street—the closest thing to an artsy district you could find in the suburbs—and drank I don't know how many double caps and talked I don't know how long. She more than held up her end of the conversation. There wasn't a subject I could bring up that she couldn't keep up on. There was nothing I liked that she didn't like, nothing I loathed that she didn't loathe. It never occurred to me to check my watch until well past eleven.

Whereupon Monica reached across the booth and unstrapped it.

"It ruined your look," she said, dangling the gaudy Swatch from a scarlet fingernail. "You're very attractive in black."

So was she, actually. More than attractive. But what had brought *that* on? "Was that a pass?"

"Was that a catch?"

Damned if I knew. I smiled uncertainly.

Monica fastened my watch onto her own wrist. "Flirt with me. We're well past the preliminaries now. Tell me I'm the woman of your dreams, and I'll tell you what happens next."

"You *are* my dreams. That's the literal truth. I know it sounds crazy, but—"

"Can I tempt you?"

I jumped. But she was merely offering to feed me a bite of her biscotti. Feeling foolish and very conspicuous, I retreated behind my cappuccino cup.

"Flirtation," she remarked, "is a lost art. Perhaps you're too literal for it. Let's move on to seduction."

I almost choked on cappuccino. "Seduction? What seduction?"

"Yours, of course."

It occurred to me that I might be in trouble. "I'm celibate. By choice. It's not that I'm not flattered, but—"

"By choice, yes. But why make that choice?"

Before I could think of anything to say to that, she reached across the booth again to rest her fingertips lightly on my wrist. "You're warm. You have a pulse. You're mortal. Do you think you have forever?"

I jerked my arm back, not wanting to feel what I'd just felt.

Unrebuffed, Monica smiled. Her eyes ran down my shirt buttons and then back up, as though she were counting them.

For control, I gripped my cup harder—and for no reason at all, it shattered, cutting one hand.

Monica leaned farther into the candlelight, red eyes glittering, to check the cut. Then, without warning, she pressed it to her mouth. I tried to pull away, but she pulled back the other way, harder.

"Christ, Monica," I whispered fiercely. "What are you *doing*?"

The other patrons of the coffeehouse had been watching us all evening, curious, but now they were starting to stare. There was going to be no explaining this. Nice normal people didn't carry on this way. Drinking blood—and in public—was too much even for Shipley Street.

"Monica, dammit, *stop* it."

"Conformist," she murmured. But she finally let go.

I moved all the way back on my side of the booth, deliberately sitting on my hands, and glared at her. For a long moment, neither of us spoke.

"You didn't even ask if I'm *tested*," I finally complained.

"You were tested," she said calmly, "on April twenty-third. At Central Hospital, on AIDS Awareness Day. On a bet. You're still negative. You taste a little anemic, though. Stress, I should think. Tell Dr. Shapiro to run a blood count the next time you—"

"How do you *know* that?"

"That your red-cell count is down?"

"That I was tested. *When* I was tested. *Where*—"

"I told you—I'm your demon. I know everything about you. Down to your blood type and your sexual fantasies. Even the ones you don't know about yet."

My mental wiring, already overloaded, began to shower sparks. My God, what a night.

"Suppose that I don't believe you," I told her. "Suppose that I don't *believe* in demons. Or angels, or any of the rest of that superstitious claptrap."

"They say that there are no atheists in the bedroom. Shall we find out?"

"I'm leaving. You're insane."

"Insanity is nothing but misdirected drive. So *you're* the one who's insane, by that definition. Tell me I'm wrong. If you can. Where do *you* fall on the Kinsey Scale?"

My shock must have shown, because she laughed, startlingly.

And then, much more startlingly, she vanished.

I knew it then: I'd been had.

CB ED

There was nothing to do after that but pay the check and start walking home. The longer I walked, the angrier I got. She'd really had me going there at the end. She was good. She was *too* good. She was a setup, as sure as I was alive.

Somebody was having some fun with me. Somebody who knew me too well, who knew that celibacy was starting to bother me, who knew exactly how to scare me. This had Cassie written all over it. Cassie *and* Kurt—which would explain that conversation in my office earlier in the week.

It added up. Advertising is the business of illusion, after all, and we all had access to the props. This Monica was an actress, of course. A good one; I'd give her that. As for the special effects—the trick with the cigarettes, the way she kept dematerializing and then rematerializing . . .

Well, those things, I couldn't explain just yet. But J/J/G had the best video department in town, and you could buy any one of those jerks for a six-pack.

They'd probably staged the dreams, too. Maybe they'd spliced subliminal images into work tapes. Everyone knew I had to look at video almost every day. They'd all gone to a lot of trouble. But they probably were wallowing in payoff now. That could've been Kurt at the coffeehouse, at the table by the far wall, in a phony beard and bald cap. No doubt he was back at the party right now, telling all.

I could almost hear him.

You should've seen Dev's face when that woman licked her. I hope the film comes out. Who wants prints?

I couldn't wait to get my hands on him—and on Cassie, too.

Furious, embarrassed, guilty as sin, I started walking faster. I'd never suspected her of having that Machiavellian streak or that kind of taste for vengeance. All I'd done—lately—was subscribe her to a really interesting podcast. Her own fault for giving me her password. She'd thrown a very satisfactory tantrum in my office the next morning. But she'd gotten over it. In fact, we'd conspired to subscribe Heather to the same podcast before the day was over.

What a devious creature Cassie was. If only she weren't so—

Evil. Some concept. Was Monica *my* concept of evil? Was it that obvious?

"To everyone but you," Cassie would say, if I were fool enough to ask. "Yes, a vampire is obvious, Devvy. Think about it. Bram Stoker was a Victorian, and Irish, and his brain was half-rotten with syphilis. He probably couldn't *help* making up vampires. What's *your* excuse?"

I didn't have one. The worst of it was that I'd wanted Monica.

No—the *very* worst of it was that I still did.

Sexual evil. All right, fine. I was obvious. I was as crazy as Bram Stoker. I was out of my box. It was time to go home.

Chapter 4
Saturday

Something—sirens? the sun?—woke me.

What time was it? I brushed just enough hair out of my eyes to see the clock on the night table, swore, and went back under the covers. No point getting up now.

Then it registered, and a quick check confirmed it: I'd gone to bed with my coat and shoes on. Would've still had my watch on, too, if Monica hadn't stolen it last night. Funny—I hadn't done that since college, after one of those damn Theta Chi parties. Last night, though, I hadn't been drinking.

Funny, too—I hadn't dreamed.

I got up and made for the bathroom. What I had in mind, in no particular order, was a shower, pajamas, and whatever was in the refrigerator. What did you call it when you had breakfast at one in the afternoon? Surely not brunch. Brunch was Bloodies at ten-thirty at some expense-account hotel, not grazing in the kitchen in last night's clothes.

Preoccupied with the question, I flipped on the bathroom light and glanced into the mirror on the medicine cabinet.

But it wasn't me in the mirror. It was Monica.

I believe that I literally jumped out of my skin. Wildly, stupidly, I slammed the medicine cabinet open and then slammed it shut again, on the chance that there was some sort of technical problem with the mirror. When I looked again, I saw my own reflection. Not an improvement, considering.

This had nothing to do with anyone from J/J/G. They

couldn't have gotten in. Cassie couldn't have *let* them in. I'd hidden the spare key somewhere else after she'd barged in the day before.

Monica might have been telling the truth. She really might be a demon.

That thought hadn't hit all the way home yet when the doorbell rang. I jumped out of my skin again.

But why would a demon bother to ring? When they come for you, don't they just *come* for you?

Well, there was only one way to find out, and the only way out was through. Drawing myself up as bravely as possible, I went downstairs to meet my fate.

Which turned out to be a stocky young man in coveralls. "Kerry?"

Puzzled, I nodded.

"Classic Auto. Got your car here."

The relief was stupendous. "My car? Already? Great. I didn't expect you till—" Then I saw what was in the driveway. "Wait. That's not my car."

Now the mechanic looked puzzled. He checked his clipboard. "Kerry? 8515 Park?"

"Yes, but that's not my car. It's a—"

"MG ragtop. Green. '73. Says so right here. Got your keys in the ignition. Sign this for me?"

Bewildered, I signed the receipt. The car in the driveway was a cherry-red Miata, as new as a shiny dime. I'd always wanted one. But this one wasn't mine. Obviously, there'd been a mixup at the shop, and equally obviously, the mechanic was blind. I'd have to have a word with his boss when I took the car back. A blind mechanic couldn't possibly be a good idea.

"Have a good one," he said, and started off to the truck parked on the street, where his driver was waiting. Suddenly, he stopped and backtracked, searching his coveralls for something. "Almost forgot. They gave me this to give you."

I took the envelope. Parchment. No logo, no return address, just my name in elegant script. From a car-repair shop? This had to be bad. The bill on the MG must have come to a fortune.

Inside the envelope, though, I found not an invoice but a parchment sheet bearing the same elegant script. It said:

> *D-*
> *You tempt beautifully. Being pleased, I send you this*
> *token of my pleasure.*
> 	*Thank me tonight.*
> 			*-M*
> *P.S.: Your watch is under your pillow.*

"Lady? You OK?"

I left the blind SOB standing on the porch. Maybe I'd drive the Miata for a couple of days, just for spite.

୧୨

Troubles have a way of coming in threes. First, the bad scare in the bathroom; second, the problem with the car. So it was no real surprise that the phone rang as soon as I closed the door. I let voice mail pick up and waited a few minutes to check it.

"Devlin? It's Susie Taylor. You know—Dr. Shapiro's receptionist? Listen, I saw you last night at the coffee-house. I don't want to upset you or anything, but I thought I ought to tell you that you were acting a little . . . well, kind of strange. Talking to somebody who wasn't even *there*, I mean. Our waiter said you were like that all night, and they were kind of humoring you, just in case you were dangerous or something.

"The reason I'm calling is I know you were in a couple of

days ago to see Dr. Shapiro, and I was wondering if you're OK. Maybe your medicine's acting funny or something. Why don't you call up and make another appointment so she can look at you again? Just to be safe? We're open till three today, if you get back in time. Thanks. Bye."

Just to verify, I played the message back. I *had* heard her right the first time.

So much for the rest of my sanity. The only thing left to do was go work out.

03&0

Even for Greenville, Club West was an architectural felony. What with all the glass and plastic, on a sunny day you could probably see the place from the moon.

Inside, it was even worse, all neon and mirrors and screaming supergraphics. Day and night, hard rock played at maximum volume, even in the locker rooms. If you happened to be on the workout floor during an aerobics class, you also got a good blast of whatever was on the instructor's boom box. Add to that the characteristic aroma of the place—a hellbrew of Ben-Gay and Giorgio—and you begin to understand the peculiar nature of an expensive health club, which is the kind of place where you shower *before* you work out.

Even so, I liked the club. Whatever else it might be, it was clean, it was bright, and it didn't smell like a gym. Moreover, it was the best-equipped health club around. I'd been working out there for years.

Besides, Club West was one of J/J/G's glamour clients, and it never hurts to keep an eye on clients.

I got there between aerobics classes, so lobby traffic was heavy. While I waited for the desk clerk to check me in—she was too busy flirting with a slack-jawed frat boy to notice me at the moment—I checked out the crowd. Nothing unusual. Nothing like my commercials, either. For every pretty boy or girl who looked good in Spandex, there were a couple dozen who didn't. Idly, I wondered for the zillionth time why so many men worked out in baseball caps. I wondered why so many women thought Public Underwear was a good look. A T-shirt and shorts were good enough to work out in. Who wanted to wear sweaty Spandex anyway?

Of course, I wore the most expensive cross-trainers on the market, and true, I was guilty of showering before workouts myself, but there was a line between being serious and being a slob.

There was also a line between being serious and being a nimrod, which was what so many members were. They fought for parking spaces right next to the door—at a health club. They fought for the lat machines—and just posed on them. They fought for the best treadmills—and strolled on them while they talked on their cell phones. Even Cassie refused to go out with men who tried to pick her up at Club West. She said the gene pool there didn't have enough lifeguards.

I brooded about all these things for a few minutes and then realized that the clerk still hadn't noticed me. She was very busy shrieking in mock outrage at something the frat boy had just said. Frowning, I tapped my card on the counter. No response.

I was about to put the card in her face physically when a tall boy in a neon-green baseball cap pushed through the front door. Waves of Polo rolled in with him. Like a trout, the desk clerk leaped to him, reaching right past me for his card.

"Hey!" I protested.

The clerk gave me the fish eye as she swiped Green Cap's card through the reader. Silently, she handed his card back and held out her hand for mine. She swiped it, dropped it on the counter as though it had cooties, and then resumed her urgent flirting, turning her back on the group of women just coming through the door.

OK, sometimes I hated Club West, too.

On the way to the locker room, I passed one of the new posters. Something about the color register caught my eye—I didn't remember the lettering being quite so red in the crom proof—so I stopped to have a closer look. Then, a little absently, I checked the rest of the artwork.

And jumped so high that I almost hit the ceiling tiles. Instead of Bouncing Betsy, the model in the poster was Monica. She was wearing the same skin-tight leotard and the same you-can-be-had expression, and there were two razor-sharp fangs in her half-smiling mouth.

I blinked and checked again. Still Monica. But now she appeared to be laughing—and she was wearing nothing at all.

It was time to run for it. In any direction. But before I could work up any speed, I crashed into a big person in a Club West shirt.

Danny. My trainer. Well, at least it was a big person I knew.

Shaking his head, he helped me off the floor. "Track's upstairs, Dev. You OK?"

I checked the poster again. Bouncing Betsy. "Yeah. I'm OK. Sorry."

"You sure? Everything all right?"

Carefully, I shifted my expression into neutral. "Yeah. Everything's fine. Thanks for the lift."

"Hey—no harm, no foul. You coming or going?"

"Coming. Then going to the office for a while. No time for a session today, Danny. Sorry."

"Soon, then. It's been a couple weeks. Give me a ring when you get the time. OK?"

I promised to do that. Then I headed straight to the locker room, with the idea of sticking my head in one of the sinks and running cold water over it until everything cleared.

Unfortunately, I couldn't even get near a sink. Six or seven college girls were lined up at the mirrors, putting on makeup *before* extended bench class.

All right, so maybe troubles come in fours and fives every so often.

☙❧

Late that afternoon, Cassie walked into my office without warning. Why didn't anybody ever knock around that place?

"We must've just missed each other at the club," she said. "Danny said you said something about coming here. He *also* said you looked funny. He was right. What happened to you last night?"

"Couldn't say," I told her, truthfully. "What are you doing here?"

"Came in to check my e-mail. But don't change the subject. I saw you out back last night talking to some strange woman. You—"

"Spying on me, were you?"

"No, I wasn't spying on you. Linda asked me to see if you were out there *relapsing* and ashing in her precious garden. So I looked out the back window, just to humor her, and there you were—with Elvira. The next time I looked, you were gone. If she'd been a guy, I'd have been worried about you. Who was she?"

I feinted. "Did you ask Greg and Linda?"

"They don't know her. They never even saw her. Apparently, I'm the only person who *did*, except for you. You really don't know who she was?"

"Sorry."

Cassie perched on the edge of my desk. Couldn't have been comfortable under all that Spandex. "But you know everything."

I didn't bite, but I studied her for a minute, trying to read her mood. She'd said that *she'd* seen Monica. Was this some sort of proof that I wasn't crazy?

"Cass? Can I ask you something?"

"Sure. What?"

"Did you see my car in the lot?"

"I did," she said. "I parked next to it."

"What does it look like to you?"

"Like it always does—like a moving violation. I keep telling you that you can afford a *real* car now."

I studied her more closely. She'd seen the MG, not the Miata, and she wouldn't have lied about it because she'd always hated the MG. How come she couldn't see the car if she could see Monica?

"You can afford a house, too, as far as that goes," Cassie continued, taking my silence for agreement. "Why you live the way you do is beyond—"

"Do you believe in witches?"

"Not since preschool. Why? Do you?"

Not sure how to answer that, I turned away from her to the window.

"Witches, Devvy. *Really*. And what would they have to do with your car anyway?"

"What about vampires?"

"Only if they're Tom Cruise," she said promptly. "What are you getting at?"

"I don't know. Forget it." I turned back around and smiled sheepishly, in apology.

But Cassie wasn't buying. "You *do* look funny. Peculiar, I mean. You've *been* looking peculiar for a couple of days now. What did Shapiro say? Did you hit your head in the wreck? Do you have a concus—?"

"I'm OK."

"You're OK." She snorted. "You're sitting here in broad

daylight, sober, asking me if I believe in witches and vampires and *goblins,* and you're OK."

"Forget it, I said. Forget I asked."

"How?"

Silence.

"That does it," Cassie said. "Go home. Go to bed. Don't even get up tomorrow. I mean it. If you're still like this on Monday, I'm taking you to *my* doctor. Shapiro's a quack. She—"

"Just because she married Dr. Right out from under you?"

"You leave me out of this. Shapiro's a mallard. If you looked up her skirt, you'd see feathers. If she had any medical training at all, she'd have shot you full of Thorazine and called Research Psychiatric. So it's up to me now, and I am *not* letting you go any crazier than you already are. Capeesh?"

I opened my mouth to talk back, but to no avail.

"Don't start with me," Cassie warned. She gave me a little shove for emphasis and then got up to leave. At the door, though, she turned. "Does any of this have anything to do with that woman last night?"

"What a question," I said coolly. "Why do you ask?"

"I don't know. But you *did* just disappear like that." She shook her head, dismissing the subject. "I'm going. Go home and get some rest."

"Hey. By the way. How was Mark last night?"

Cassie smiled wryly. "I'm thinking about putting a sticker on my bra: 'Some Foreplay Required.'"

"There's always celibacy."

"Don't try to recruit *me,* you pervert. See you Monday."

Maybe, I thought, and went back to reading the fine print in my disability policy.

CHAPTER 5
SATURDAY NIGHT

The sun was almost down when I pulled into the driveway and switched off the engine. I wasn't sure that I wanted to commit as far as the garage. Monica might already be inside, waiting, and who knew what would happen then?

So I waited too, watching the last of the daylight disappear in the dark windows of the condo. A light wind began to stir, just enough to flutter a neighbor's wind chimes; black thunderheads stacked up over the tree line; birds twittered in the burning bushes and then fell silent. By the feel of things, we were in for a nasty storm.

Unwillingly, I started the car again—the top was down, and I didn't know how to put it up—and pressed the button on the garage-door opener. The door creaked and groaned like something out of the House of Usher. All that was missing now, I figured, was Vincent Price.

But just when I'd half-decided to spend the night at a motel, Cassie's mocking comment came back to me—*witches and vampires and goblins*. She probably would've told me I was just trying to scare myself. She probably would've been right.

Besides, Monica had sent this sexy little car. Even if I was the only person who could see it, the least I could do was thank her. I couldn't keep it, but at least I could thank her.

So I garaged the Miata and walked cautiously into the dark condo.

Well, it wasn't totally dark. The lights were off, as they should have been. But the minute I stepped in, a fire roared to life in the greatroom fireplace.

Damn, I've seen this movie.

"Monica?"

No answer.

"I know you're here. Where are you?"

No answer. Fine. She wanted to play games, apparently. She probably wanted to make some kind of grand entrance—in a pillar of fire, no doubt. Who was I to stop her?

Muttering, I slung my club bag into the laundry room and went to the kitchen to pour a brandy. With any luck, there'd be enough brandy to last the night.

Halfway to the greatroom, I saw the shadow.

"Monica?"

"Devlin."

She was curled up against one arm of the couch. Uncertain, I stayed put.

"About the car," I said tentatively.

"Yes. Do you like it?"

"Like it? I love it. I wish I could live in it. . . . I can't accept it, Monica. But thanks for the thought. It was really—"

"It pleased me to give it to you. It would please me to have you accept it."

"But it's not real. Is it?"

"It's real. But it'll be our little secret for now. You want it, don't you?"

She had me there. Besides, maybe it was real enough. Maybe demons *could* conjure up little red cars just like that. So why not take it? If it would please her . . .

"All right. Thank you. I accept."

"Accept this, too." She reached over to the coffee table, where she'd set up bar, after a fashion, and poured some sort of liqueur into a crystal stem.

"Thanks, but I've already got—"

"I insist. Take it."

Shrugging, I took it and had a good look at the contents. Nothing I could identify, but nothing identifiably lethal, either.

Monica finished pouring her own drink and then stood— perhaps too close. "To beginnings."

Beginnings? Well, all right. Why not?

We touched stems lightly and drank. Whatever the liqueur was, it was first-class goods. I started to ask her about it, but her expression made me stop short. She was studying me minutely, with those strange lights glinting in her eyes, and she really *was* standing too close.

"Do you have a last name?" I asked, uneasy.

"Yours, if you like. Why do you ask? Do I need one?"

"Well, it would be normal. Or at least more nor—"

"Normal. How clever of you to bring that up. What *is* normal?"

Something cold shot up my spine. Trying to make it look casual, I moved away from her, all the way over to the fireplace.

She understood, and laughed. The cold shot up again, stronger this time.

"Who are you?" I asked.

"Who do you think I am?"

"Dammit, Monica, I'm serious."

"Yes. You *are* serious. You're starting to think that you're afraid of me." Slowly, she moved closer. "You're still not quite sure that I'm not a special effect. You're seeing things that you think aren't there. You're having dreams that you can't explain. You're starting to doubt your sanity. Not to mention your sexuality." There was complete certainty in her tone, and a note of mockery. "Do you believe in witches, Devlin?"

That really did it. I set my stem down hard on the mantel. "I think I should leave now."

But suddenly Monica was one step away, and she took it. Then her mouth was on mine, kissing very slowly, at exquisite leisure, as though she had all the time there was and needed no permission whatsoever.

Can you imagine what that was like after six years of celibacy? But with a woman?

A beautiful woman, though, warm, real, apparently quite willing. It *had* been six years. And against all odds—not to mention every law of God and man—it felt . . . right.

But with a woman?

Yes, she was undeniably a woman, and I'd undeniably wanted her all along. *First-class passage to Hell*, I thought, and closed my eyes, and gave in.

No sooner had I done so, though, than she released me. "You're free to go now, if you like."

I didn't move. Her lips curved into an ambiguous smile.

"Remember that you were afraid and that you had your chance to leave. Dinner?"

CSSO

Dinner, which was already waiting in the dining room, was extraordinary. Two wines, seven courses, and nothing I didn't like—which, for someone who'd been known to live on spaghetti for weeks, was extraordinary too. To my surprise, I'd been starving.

By the time we got to dessert, the edge was off. But only the edge. She laughed and pushed her untouched cheesecake over to me. "So there *are* pleasures that you enjoy."

"Not this. Not usually. Food's just fuel, usually. But this . . ." At a loss for a word that would be enormous enough, I gave up and dug into the cheesecake.

"You've been denying yourself for a very long time. Such a shame. Such a waste." Her voice was light, casual, almost like

Cassie's when she was working up to goad me. "You must find advertising difficult. Being in the business of temptation, and yet not being tempted."

So we were back to that. I put down my fork—grudgingly—and waited.

"Life must be terribly bleak for you. Food is fuel, and sex is business. When it's not sin, that is. I wonder what you think sin is. An appetite is an appetite. Have you committed a sin here tonight?"

Very likely. The cheesecake alone was almost certainly a million calories. To work it off, I'd have to do an extra half-hour on the stair machine every day for the next couple of weeks. Or an extra half-hour every day for a week if I added five pounds on all the circuit machines I used, and maybe added a set of reps to—

"Mortifying your flesh again," Monica said dryly. "How inconvenient that you're not Catholic."

I didn't much like this mind-reading business but decided to try to make a joke of it. "Catholics don't belong to Club West. It leads to birth control."

"You have all of the guilt, but none of the redemption. You're very guilty. Why?"

"You tell me. You say you know everything about—"

"Celibacy is just your expiation for your guilt. Your Irish Catholic Methodist atheist form of expiation. You *are* tempted, but you deny it. You deny yourself. Who told you that what tempts you is necessarily a sin?"

That question brought me up short. I'd always thought the evil of temptation was self-evident. But was it really? And who *had* told me?

"Think," she demanded.

I thought—and then the coin dropped. "Genesis. Of *course*. I had a book when I was six years old. A children's Bible, with pictures. I remember the Genesis part especially. Nice detail on the snake, but all you saw of God was the feet. He must be a big son of a—"

"Tell me about temptation, the way you learned it when you were six years old. According to Genesis, with pictures."

"It's only a story. A dumb one. I thought so even when I was little. How anyone old enough to tie his own shoes can still believe it is a mystery to me. Even a fundie with a grade-school education should be able to see through—"

"Never mind that right now," she said. "Just tell me the story. As you know it."

"As *I* know it, it's just a lot of nonsense about snakes and apples and some great big killjoy in sandals called Yahweh. *Yahweh*, for God's sake. Couldn't the Creator of Everything come up with a better name for himself? No wonder the world doesn't work. *Yahweh*." Scornfully, I drained my liqueur stem and then refilled it. "It's a stupid story. For stupid people. Sometimes I think Genesis is responsible for half the evil in the world."

Monica's eyes lighted up. "Real evil? Or sexual evil?"

What kind of question was that? "Evil, period. I think whoever wrote Genesis must have hated women. And snakes. *And* rationality. But my God, do people believe it. 'It ain't written,'" I said, slipping into my best white-trash accent. "'It ain't in the Good Book that God made Adam and Steve. So it ain't fittin.' 'Sides which, it ain't moral. *'Sides* which, I ain't gettin' any.'"

"Old joke."

"Old story. These people are hilljacks."

"Don't call yourself names."

That lost me. "What?"

"Simple Aristotelian logic. A: All Bible-believers are hilljacks . . . to use your word. B: All sexual difference is contrary to the Bible. Ergo, C: All those who believe that sexual difference is evil are hilljacks."

"There's something wrong with that syllogism," I said. "Besides, you can't put me in it, because I don't believe the Bible."

"You lie like an expert."

I regarded her narrowly. "I *am* an expert. But I'm not lying right now. I don't believe—"

"You don't believe, and yet you won't disbelieve. You won't sin, and yet you don't stop wanting to. What holds you back? What are you afraid of? Genesis?"

"Revelation."

It was only a joke. But Monica took it seriously.

"Revelation comes in many shapes, Devlin. I'm the shape of yours."

"Who are you? The truth."

"Your demon."

"The *truth*, dammit."

"Your demon. Shall I prove it?"

෫෬෭

She led the way upstairs to what had been my bedroom, the last time I saw it. What it was now was anyone's guess—a set from a Fellini movie, maybe. Red-satin-draped walls. Black carpeting; black curtains. A forest of candelabra, with all the candles burning. Black mirrors on the walls. And an enormous mahogany bed, all carving and polish, with a red canopy, red hangings, and what appeared to be red silk sheets.

"Great God," I muttered. "Who's your decorator?"

Monica smiled slightly. "Derivative. I agree. But who am I to disappoint you?"

"We haven't established who you are, period."

"You haven't been listening. You want a simple answer, so I've given you one. This is it. Your snake, in your Garden."

I had to think about that one for a second. "I think you're

mixing your metaphors. What kind of demon are you? Theological? Or psychological?"

"Is there a difference?"

"What are you saying?"

"Just what I was saying before. Shall I say it again?"

"I don't understand. Are you telling me that you're *real*?"

"I'm very real. I'm what you're most afraid of. What did you think a demon was?"

Good question. I'd supposed that the horns and the pointy tail came into play somewhere, but I'd never given it any serious thought. Still . . .

"Who *are* you? What are you doing here?"

"You know who I am, and I'm doing what you should have done for yourself a long time ago. You've called me. You can't deny me now. You want me. And what you want, sooner or later, you have to have."

As she spoke, she moved closer, opening her gown as she advanced. By the time she reached me, the gown was open to the waist. Uncomfortable, I looked away. But she took my hand and placed it inside.

Oh, God. She was real, all right. But . . .

"OK. Maybe I *do* want you some," I admitted, jerking my hand back. "You're very convincing. You might even be real. But then again, you might just be a rationalization of some sort. Or a fantasy. I can't get involved with a fantasy. It would look bad."

"I'm not a fantasy. Give me your hand again."

"Why?"

For answer, she just took it and put it back where it was before. This time, she held it there.

"Where did I get you from?" I asked helplessly. "Anne Rice?"

Monica didn't answer. She moved much closer.

Very uncomfortable now, I stepped backward and tried to

hold her at bay. "All right. OK. Suppose that I believe you, for just a second, just for the sake of argument. You're a demon, or something that I've been repressing, and somehow, you got out. Stranger things could happen. Maybe. But what happened that you got out? Why now?"

"Why not?"

While I searched for an answer to that, she closed the distance between us again, pulled me to her, and kissed me. For quite some time. With increasing heat. I was forgetting what objections I'd had to this in the first place.

"Maybe we should go to bed," I told her, "while my motor skills still work."

"We're not going to bed. Not tonight."

I jumped as though I'd been shot. "What do you mean, we're not—?"

"Not yet. Come here."

"What do you want? My soul? Done. It's yours. No questions asked. I don't even care if you're real. All right? Do we have a deal?"

"You still need tempting."

"I do not. I absolutely do not. I'm . . . where are you going?"

She had suddenly moved away, out of reach, and was smiling rather appraisingly at me.

"Dammit, Monica, what are you—?"

The words froze on my lips. I'd been talking to Monica, but now *Cassie* was standing in front of me: Cassie, in Monica's black gown, open to the waist, with an appraising expression in her blue eyes. She took a step toward me . . .

. . . and I bolted from the bedroom to the garage to the car. I didn't stop for a single red light until the next county.

Chapter 6
Even Later Saturday Night

Dr. Shapiro walked into the emergency room in a fancy dress and a temper. "Valium? You gave her that much Valium?"

"You weren't here when she came in, Doctor," the intern told her. "She was agitated. She said something about a devil and burning in Hell. I thought—"

"Thank you," she said curtly. "She's my patient. I'll do the thinking from now on."

The intern bit his lip and bowed out, closing the curtains behind him.

"Night," I called from the exam table. "Thanks for the drugs."

Shaking her head, Shapiro checked my chart again. "Valium. By injection. May I assume that you're feeling more relaxed now?"

"Much. No thanks to you. What are you doing here?"

"They paged me. What are *you* doing here?"

"Nerves. I was going to call you Monday. . . . Hey, great dress, Doc. Did the shoes come with it?"

"Let's just talk about your symptoms, shall we? I understand that you saw the Devil tonight. Is that why you're nervous? I shouldn't wonder. Are you taking the BuSpar?"

"Should I be?"

She sighed. "I can't help you if you won't take your medicine. There's nothing more I can do for you tonight. Go home. Call a taxi; you're in no condition to drive. And—"

"I want the other doctor back," I said sulkily. "He was nice. He was interested. He took notes. Did I ever tell you that a lot of people think you're a quack?"

Shapiro didn't answer. She was writing something on a prescription pad. When she finished, she tore off the top sheet and handed it to me. "Fill this in the morning. Call Monday for an appointment. I think we'll have you CAT-scanned. Meanwhile, if you see any little red men with pitchforks, remind yourself that you were in a car accident a few days ago. You may have subdural trauma of some sort. Anything else?"

"I can't read this."

"You're not supposed to. Go home now." She pulled back the curtains and checked her watch. "I may just get back in time for the Schumann."

"Quack!" I shouted after her.

Then I tore up the prescription, climbed down from the exam table, and wobbled out of the ER to the car, which I drove at a cool 10 mph all the way home.

ଔୃ

Despite the Valium, the dream routed me off the couch in the middle of the night—I wasn't about to set foot in that bedroom—so I gave up and got up to make coffee . . . and to pace around the living room and sulk some more.

I wondered how Shapiro had managed to get those ankle-strap pumps on over her webs. How she'd managed to get out of residency without being arrested for impersonation or murder. Monica was no subdural trauma—she'd caused the wreck. She'd come first—and all the prescriptions in the world weren't going to make her go away. I'd been a fool to go to the emergency room.

Telling the truth had been out of the question, of course. *I've had this subconscious sexual fantasy, Doc. She says she's my demon. She got out somehow, and she's after me. What have you got for that?*

Riiiight. The med-school profs probably told them to call 911 when they heard stories like that. And not even the stump-dumb cops of Greenville would believe this one—assuming that anyone could flush them out of the doughnut shops long enough to listen.

Telling a minister would be impossible, too, and not just because I wasn't a Believer. Where would I find a minister in this county on a Saturday night, anyway? All the Right Revs would be at home in the bosoms of their families, playing hymns on the Kimball, or out wenching and brawling in the bars.

There was always Cassie, but telling her was even further out of the question. Even if she believed me—which she wouldn't, but even if she did—she'd just tell me it was my own fault for being celibate for so long.

I wondered whether Cassie believed in anything like sin . . . and whether she knew *I* knew that she wasn't half as loose as she let on. She liked to outrage me whenever she could, though, and she was very, very good at it. Monday morning, she'd have some towering lie to tell me about her wild night tonight.

Her night would be nine-tenths work, in perfect truth. She was going to Rumours to have another look around. She knew that I wasn't making much progress, but I knew she'd lie if the owners asked her how the campaign was coming.

"Don't worry," she'd say. "Devvy's the best. She's working on something that'll make grown men lock themselves in the bathroom. You'll have to run the spots on cable at two in the morning, with disclaimers. I guarantee that your business is going to triple. If you see her, will you tell her I had group sex in the middle of the dance floor?"

Bemused, I went back to the kitchen to pour a drink,

thinking about crazy blondes and Baptist morality and certain damnation. I'd just uncorked a bottle when the idea came, clear and complete.

I had the Rumours campaign, and Jack would love it.

To make sure, I ran the footage in my head again. Then I raced upstairs to the master bath to shower and dress. I could be at the office in fifteen minutes if the lights were with me.

CHAPTER 7
MONDAY

Cassie threw open my office door, without knocking, to catch me drinking coffee straight out of the carafe. "Devvy!"

Guilty, I jumped, spilling coffee on my shirt. No real damage—it was a day old, and it was black. The shirt, I mean. Still . . .

I checked Cassie's expression. She was looking at me as though I were from Pluto.

"It may be time for us to have a long talk about decaf," she finally said. "Or about the Betty Ford Center, if they *have* a coffee program. You may even want to consider—"

"Don't start with me. It's not even nine yet. Why are *you* here?"

"I had a breakfast meeting with a client. Why are you here?"

People had been asking that question for days, it seemed, and I was beginning to resent it. So I ignored her and took the carafe back to my desk.

"If I thought you'd slept," she continued, "I'd say you look like you slept in those clothes. What in the world have you been doing?"

"Working. Couldn't sleep, so I came in to work. This idea came to me, and—"

"What time couldn't you sleep? What day?"

I considered. "I don't know. But never mind. Since you're here—"

"I'm calling my doctor. This minute."

"Whatever. But come here first. I want you to look at this."

"What is it?"

"A storyboard. Nobody was in Illustration, so I had to draw it myself. So it's crude. But take a look anyway."

"What's it for?"

"Rumours," I said.

Still suspicious, Cassie took the storyboard. For a long time, she didn't say anything.

Finally, I couldn't stand it anymore. "So? What do you think?"

"Risky."

"I know. But—"

"Very risky."

"Right. But do you think it'll fly?"

Cassie smiled. Relieved, I sank back into my chair.

"Oh, it'll fly," she said, "and I want to pitch it. Let me run it past Jenner for you."

"You can't do that. I have to have Jack sign off."

"Trust me—you need me for this one. Never mind Jack. I'll go over his head."

Evidently the chain of command wasn't the only thing that she didn't understand. "*You* can't take this to Jenner, dammit. *I* did the creative."

"You don't like him."

"Neither do you."

"Neither do his wives," she agreed, "or his girlfriends, or his hookers. But I don't have to sleep with him."

"He wants to sleep with you." Jenner wanted to sleep with every woman, actually, and he was trying to do just that. But he'd always had a particular thing for Cassie, and only her sweet recitals of sexual-harassment law kept him on his own side of the desk when she was around. "You're going to go up and see him with *that* dress on?"

She laughed and examined her figure under the Italian knit. "I like this dress. It's lucky."

"For who?"

"It's just insurance, baby duck. Jenner's never going to get anywhere with me. But can I help it if I know he likes to look?"

Sadly, I shook my head. Cassie was shameless . . . and very, very good at getting what she wanted. While I pondered her dark art, she picked up my phone and called Jenner's admin.

"Five minutes," she told me, pressing the switchhook before she dialed again. "Beth? It's Cassie Wolfe. I'm in Dev Kerry's office. Could you send somebody here to photocopy a storyboard for me? On a color copier? . . . Right away. I've got to see Jenner in five minutes. . . .Yes. Thanks." She hung up. "Anything you want while I'm up there?"

"You're going to get caught one of these days. He's dumb, but he may not be terminal."

"Don't bet your life." She mussed my hair. "We make a good team, even though I don't like you. We ought to have our own agency, just like on 'thirtysomething.' Remember? The Michael & Elliot Company? We'll call ours The Cassie & Devvy Company."

"The Devvy & Cassie Company," I corrected. "And they went broke on 'thirtysomething,' remember?"

"Fiction," she said airily.

One of the interns arrived at that point to pick up the storyboard. We discussed percentage of reduction, degree of contrast, size of paper until I realized that he wasn't listening. He was too busy reviewing Cassie's insurance.

"Today," I suggested.

The boy nodded, backing away with the storyboard so he could keep gawking at Cassie as long as possible—and tripped over a wastebasket for his trouble.

I scowled first at him and then at her. "You may be carrying too much coverage, Cass."

Her only response was a smirk. Sometimes, the woman was impossible.

⊂౩౸⊃

I'd just called Kurt and Heather in for a short standup when the local line buzzed. Jenner.

"One second, sir. My copywriters are here. Will it be all right if I put you on speakerphone?"

Not getting a definite answer, I put him on speakerphone anyway. Jenner continued to yammer away—some howling madness about how exciting the concept was. It was a meaningless word, because all concepts around that place were exciting, and interesting, too; "interesting" was a Chinese curse.

The man had three speeds: Manic; Depressive; and Quick, Get the Butterfly Net. He was cruising along in the third or fourth gear of the bad speed at the moment.

"—your concept," he was saying. "Very exciting. Risky. Cutting-edge. Miss Wolfe just called the clients from here. They're on their way over. We'll have the pitch up here in fifteen."

"Sir? Excuse me—I'm going to pitch *today*? With *that* storyboard?"

"Not you. Miss Wolfe and I. She says you look like something that came in with the tide. She thinks you'll scare the clients. So we're going to keep you out of sight. Understood?"

"Yes, sir. Whatever you say." *Whatever you bleat, you old goat. Where are your hands right now?*

"Hello? Miss Devlin? Are you there?"

Kurt and Heather snickered. I gave them a silent warning. Seven years I'd worked for the man, and he still couldn't get a grip on my name. "Still here, Mr. Jenner."

"Miss Wolfe says you were here all night. She thinks you should take the day off. I think we can spare you. Is that clear?"

"Yes, sir. But—"

The phone clicked down on the other end.

"She's wearing the peach dress, isn't she?" Heather asked. "Did you tell her to tell him to give us raises?"

೫೫

When I got home, there was no sign of Monica—and I checked everywhere, just to make sure. Even my bedroom was back to normal. Some protection seemed to be in order, though. Did I have a crucifix anywhere? Any garlic? Or wolfsbane? Well, no. One Easter when I was little, we got glow-in-the-dark plastic crosses in Sunday school, but I'd never had a crucifix per se, and I had no clue what wolfsbane even was. I did, however, find garlic salt in the kitchen and was not too proud to sprinkle some around the bed before I turned in.

Late in the afternoon, I was en route from the bathroom back to bed when the doorbell rang. Just what I needed—an account manager in a lucky peach dress, bearing takeout Chinese.

"I gave at the office," I told her, and started to close the door.

Cassie put her foot in it, though, and outleaned me. Then she invaded my privacy the rest of the way.

"I'm in my pajamas!" I protested.

"Why? Were you sleeping?"

"Of course I was sleeping. Who wears pajamas when they're not sleeping? Who do I look like—Hugh Hefner?"

"You're a little prettier. But not much. Were you in bed?"

"I was on my way when—"

"Then don't let me interrupt you," she said, pushing past me.

"Wait a minute. I never asked you to—"

"We signed the contract with Rumours half an hour ago. You'll never believe what we're billing. And we're both getting bonuses out of it, because I told Jenner that bonuses would be *sweet* of him. Come on. We're celebrating this."

Outmaneuvered, I gave up and followed her back up the stairs to my bedroom. Cassie opened the bottles of Chinese beer, and we had Szechuan, with chopsticks, out of cartons, on my bed. After a while, we turned on the little TV and watched commercials with the sound off so that we could do our own narration. Then Cassie entertained me by acting out the pitch meeting. She played all the parts. She did a great Jenner.

"This is the most fun I've had in bed in six years," I remarked.

Cassie laughed. "I'm working on it, Devvy."

CS&ED

She finally left around midnight. She'd helped me clean up, though, and she'd even vacuumed, sort of, and if there was anything we'd missed, I'd worry about it tomorrow.

Weary, I got into bed, turned out the light, and rolled over—right into someone.

"Alone at last," Monica crooned. "Sleepy?"

I rocketed across the room, where it might be safer.

"Not sleepy?"

"You've got to stop this," I told her shakily. "You're making me crazy."

"You're making yourself crazy. You'll feel better if you let it out."

"You *are* out."

In the half-dark, I saw her sit up. "Great Satan, you're literal. Relax. Don't fight yourself so hard. You're human. You can't help what you want."

"But I can help what I do about it."

"Can you?" she asked, amused, and switched on the bedside lamp.

My heart slammed against my ribs so hard that it may have cracked one. She was wearing a black-lace X-rated number, and not much of it, but enough to stop a speeding train.

"Tempted?" she asked.

Yes, I was, after all, come to think of it, now that she mentioned it, and we weren't going to play this game anymore. Determined to end the temptation once and for all, I leaped into the bed.

She was gone before I landed.

CHAPTER 8
SEPTEMBER

It began with dancing.

It was black and white, like an art movie, and the dancers were almost inhumanly beautiful. A few seconds in, they began to focus on the camera, to beckon the viewer closer, to all but make love through the lens.

Then the Europop dance track stopped, and the screen went black. White capitals appeared on the black background: EVERYTHING YOU'VE HEARD IS TRUE.

Kurt tried hard to catch my eye. I ignored him, intent on Jenner, who continued to watch the screen. He was in the catatonic phase of his depressive cycle that day, or at least for the moment.

The Europop started again, the lettering vanished, and a moving image bled through the black. Then another. Then others. A man with a man; a woman with a woman; a man with two women; three men with two men. An androgynous couple, silhouetted against a bright light, moved into kiss range, both mouths open. At the critical moment, the screen went black again.

THE SNAKE REALLY DOES HAVE ALL THE LINES, the white capitals proclaimed.

Consummated kiss, with a flicker of tongue.

AT LEAST, ON THE DANCE FLOOR.

"Jesus on the dashboard," Chip whispered. Jenner continued to watch the screen.

When the music and movement started again, something shadowy was happening—something sexual, clearly, but not clearly enough. It looked like . . . could *not* be, on American television, but really looked like . . .

TEMPTED? the white capitals asked.

Two seconds of silence, followed by the Rumours logo and phone number in blazing red on the black. The end.

Absolute silence fell over the conference room. Jenner remained fixed on the screen, which was showing only static now. He neither moved nor gave any indication that he would again, ever. At the back of the room, someone coughed.

Say something, I silently told Jenner. *Nobody's going to say anything until you do.*

The back of his expensively styled gray head didn't respond.

Yes or no, damn you. They won't know what they think until you tell *them what they think.*

"Yes," Jenner said.

Around me, everyone breathed. Having known the man longer than most of them, I waited.

"This is thirty seconds, Miss Devlin?"

He was speaking to the screen, so I spoke to the back of his head. "Twenty-eight-five, sir. We left in some margin so we could give or take on the titles."

"Give me one-five more in the second segment. Leave the titles alone. What about the fifteen?"

"Most of the cut's off the top. Six seconds there, three in the middle, a couple—"

"I'll see it in my office."

"Yes, sir."

Quiet again. Finally, Jenner stood, turned, smoothed his pinstripes, and nodded at Jack, who was grinning like a cat.

"We're going to have lawyer trouble, Harper," Jenner told him. "I'll see you in my office. Bring the tape."

"Right behind you, sir," Jack said happily.

I was standing in Jenner's path to the door, but he didn't acknowledge me in the slightest as he went by. Neither did Jack. Not until the door closed behind them did anyone else move.

Then they were all moving in all directions at once, asking pointless questions. How much had it cost? Who directed, and where? How were we going to do this campaign on radio? Weren't homoerotic fantasies supposed to be out of my range?

I left the room without a word.

⋘⋙

Around seven that evening, I knocked off work and went straight home, too tired to care about anything anymore. Dr. Shapiro had finally prescribed a few sleeping pills—"just to get me through this project," I'd pleaded—and I had every intention of taking a couple and going straight to bed.

I could sleep on my own now, though, if I tried hard enough. Monica hadn't troubled my dreams for a month. I hadn't even seen her since the night she'd appeared in my bed—not so much as a pair of glittering red eyes in the rear-view mirror. She was gone as though she'd never come.

Maybe that was best. I'd had a month now to grapple with the probable truth: She'd been a hallucination. I'd pulled a Pygmalion on myself and fallen for something that didn't even exist.

Probably that was why I couldn't write anymore: I'd channeled all my creative energy into hallucinating her and had simply tapped it out. I'd shot my bolt. I'd used her up.

Or vice versa.

Listless, I pulled the car into the garage, unlocked the inside door of the condo, and walked in . . .

. . . straight into the vampire bedroom, which should have been upstairs if it should have been there at all. There wasn't time to worry about the physics of the situation, though: Monica was lying in the big mahogany bed, wearing a black silk robe open over the X-rated lace. Her smile was all sex, and her eyes were glowing like coals.

There's nothing worse than a derivative hallucination.

"At last. Welcome home," it said. "Can I tempt you?"

"What do you want?"

"You might be surprised. Come here and find out."

I complied but stopped a couple of feet from the bed.

"Closer," Monica urged.

"No. I can see you just fine from here."

"But you can't touch me, and you know you want to. You've been thinking about me all day. All month, really. So here I am. I'm all yours. Tonight's the night."

"Tonight's Tuesday," I pointed out. "People don't have sex in Greenville on Tuesday. It's a town ordinance."

She laughed. "Touchy. Maybe even a little hostile. Well, we know what causes that, don't we? Come here. You'll feel better when I'm through with you."

"You're *already* through with me. You got what you wanted when you wrote that ad for me. Didn't you?"

"Let's just say that I helped."

"So now you're going to try to get me to act on it, and you'll disappear again the minute I try to. No, thanks. I'm not that big a fool."

"You're a much bigger fool than you know. Now come here. You've kept me waiting long enough."

"For what? My soul? Are you going to bite a hole in me somewhere? Do you get the soul out that way?"

Monica got out of bed and slipped her arms around me. "There are easier ways. Tell me you want me."

"I don't want you."

"Liar." She bent down, took my top shirt button between her teeth, and bit it off.

I didn't react.

She put the tip of her tongue in my ear and unbuttoned the next button down.

Again, I didn't react. But it took all my control. I hoped that she didn't know that.

Suddenly, she pulled back. She studied me for a second—and then smiled, the fangs slowly growing longer and sharper in her red mouth.

My reaction this time was an immediate stab of fear. The next instant, Monica was on me, fangs bristling, pushing me down into the bed.

"Hate me," she demanded.

"What are you doing?"

"Hate me." She ripped my shirt open, showering buttons all over the room. "I'll ruin you. You'll lose your job. You'll lose your friends. You'll be through in this town. But you can't live without me anymore, and you know it." She slashed my khakis to ribbons with her fingernails and began to tear away the strips.

"You're insane!"

"*You're* insane. You need me. How dare you deny me?"

I tried to sit up, but she had too much leverage. "You coward. You conformist." She began to rip my shirt apart. "*Hate* me. I'm evil. I'm everything that they lie to you about. Do you hate me? Do you want me?"

I did. By then, absolutely, I did. So I pulled her down and kissed her with purpose. She responded with even greater purpose. Her mood was contagious. As I unrobed her, the silk somehow tore to shreds.

"I hate you," I whispered. "I *hate* you."

Monica wrapped herself around me, and we rolled through the bed, which seemed to be the size of the world . . .

And that was the beginning of the end of my celibacy.

⚘

I was lying flat on my back, backward in bed, wearing a strange black silk robe, and there was wind in my hair, which couldn't be right. It took a second to figure out that the bedroom window was open, that the bedroom was otherwise back to normal—and that I was very much alone.

I knew from feng shui that I shouldn't be lying with my head in that direction. But a person who'd just spent the night with a demon had specifically Western problems at the moment.

Damn. I was hers now body and soul, if she wanted, and was willing to say so. Out loud. Emphatically. I could still feel every second of the night, and the pain was nothing compared with the pleasure. It seemed that I was human after all.

I stretched, carefully, to see whether everything still worked, and felt something silk wadded up near my head: another black robe, still warm. A wave of longing swept over me. Whoever she was, whatever she was, I wanted this woman, and I—

Wait. This woman. I'd just spent the night with a woman. And if I'd done *that* with her, what did that make me?

I was in trouble, because all of a sudden, I didn't care.

⚘

What a morning. What a glorious morning. Tornado warnings outside, meetings all day inside, not a second of sleep, and I felt fantastic. Everyone I passed in the hall seemed to be astonished by my mood, for some reason, but what did it matter?

Kurt's door was open, so I stopped in to say hello. He seemed to be astonished, too.

"Something wrong, boss?"

"Wrong? Don't talk crazy. What would be wrong?"

Mistrustful, he buzzed the front desk. "Page Cassie Wolfe. Tell her—"

"I already heard," Cassie said from the doorway, "and now I see. What happened?"

"No clue," Kurt told her. "It might be a pod person."

Frowning, Cassie stepped up to get a closer look. "Are you feeling all right, Devvy?"

"Terrific. Never better. You? How about the Pig & Whistle after work?"

She told me to go away and let her think. So I left.

Through the open door, I heard Cassie mutter, "If I didn't know better, I'd say she got laid."

I had to laugh.

CHAPTER 9
LATER

My life, which had already been complicated enough, became positively Byzantine over the course of the next two or three weeks, and as the novelty of the situation began to wear off, so did some of the fun of it. Being teased by a demon had been bad, but sleeping with one was worse. She had said at the start that I was very guilty about nothing. Now I had all kinds of something to be guilty about, thanks to her, and no one to absolve me.

Don't misunderstand—it wasn't just about sex. In fact, it wasn't really about sex at all: I was beginning to see what people saw in it. Monica might be a little sharp here and there, but a few cuts and scratches were nothing to complain about compared with the rest. Besides, she said she was doing me a favor by mortifying my flesh for me. She was probably right.

No, the problem was how I felt out in the world, in daylight, among normal people. I had a terrible secret now, and it weighed on me like a stone.

It wasn't that Monica wasn't being discreet—for her. I'd begged her to please, please, *please* not out me, and she'd agreed. That wasn't necessary yet, she said, and besides, secrecy suited her purposes right now. I couldn't get her to explain the "yet" or the "right now," but I'd decided to settle for that.

We had a deal of sorts: She would appear only to me, only at night, in private, and in exchange, I would go along with whatever she wanted. At first, I'd worried about my end of the deal. But nothing bizarre ever happened, so I figured that the very fact of my sleeping with her was bizarre enough.

I wasn't really safe, though. I was still afraid of Monica, and I was even more afraid of what people would think if they found out about her.

I was sleeping with a woman. What did that make me?

I was starting to worry about that question again. I'd become uncomfortably aware of the company that people might think I was in, if word ever got out . . . so to speak.

Hypocrite? All right, OK, maybe I was. But the funny thing was, I didn't feel that way. The stereotype was the problem, and I knew very well that a stereotype doesn't get to be one without a reason. What else was advertising about, after all? As far as Meridian at large, J/J/G in small, and I in particular knew, all gay women looked like men, and therefore were not women at all. Good God, look at Connie the Barbarian. I may not have been Barbie, exactly, but I was certainly not Ken, so I wasn't one of Them. A woman, after all, was somebody like, say . . . well, Monica.

With whom I was sleeping. Damn. And it was sensational. Damn.

And the vicious circle kept turning.

⊛

With all that racket going on in my head, I didn't need any extra static from Kurt—which he probably knew, which was probably why he was being so difficult, even for him. Not long after my first post-celibate night, he started making trouble.

Heather and Troy were in my office to discuss a print ad one morning when he walked in uninvited.

"It can't be drugs," he said without preface. "You don't even smoke anymore."

"Get out of my office, Kurt," I ordered.

"It can't be multiple personalities, either, because you don't have a primary one. No, I think it has to be something sexual."

I narrowed my eyes to slits and counted to ten. Monica had pushed most of my buttons last night, and now Kurt was working on the few that she'd missed. As much as I wanted to kill something today, I didn't want blood on my office carpet.

"You're getting to be a goddamn bore, Kurt," Troy complained.

"You have a better theory?"

"No, but—"

Just to be safe, I counted to ten again. "We don't have time for this. The client wants to see a mockup tonight. So make yourself gone."

Not troubled by not being welcome, Kurt leaned back against a wall, planning to stay a while. "That's exactly the trouble—you don't have time for this. But you don't have time because you don't *make* time. My God, boss, that can be dangerous. The human sex drive comes right from the reptile brain, and you don't want to cross the reptile."

I decided to try counting in French this time, just to hold my own interest.

"Kurt," Heather protested, "we're busy."

"You don't think she's been acting funny lately?"

"Yes. But so have you."

Grateful for the defense, I smiled at her. She shrugged.

"We're working here," I reminded Kurt. "Don't make me throw you out. I really don't want to have to touch you. Don't you have something to do? Aren't you supposed to be helping Paula on the Holloway account today?"

"She's at a doctor's appointment right now. My guess is that it's about birth control. Ever since she started seeing Jack, *she's* been acting funny, too." He grinned unpleasantly. "And Jack'll be walking funny if his wife ever finds out, with that baby on the way and all. But you're getting me off my point. Which is—"

"Five seconds, Kurt," I warned, losing patience.

"—that all strange behavior has a sexual basis. That's the reptile part. The way I see it, boss, your reptile is sick, if not downright—"

A couple of critical fuses blew in my brain, and the next thing anyone knew, I had Kurt by the collar, pinned flat against the wall.

"I told you celibacy was unnatural," Kurt said, as though nothing had happened.

"This is personal," I growled. "Not professional. So don't even think about running to Jack, even if he sent you. If you say one more word about my sex life—"

Kurt's eyes lit up. "You mean you have one?"

Troy and Heather groaned. I tightened my hold on his collar. "Ow!"

"One more word, of any kind," I warned him, "and I'll put you right through this wall. I'm mad enough to do it. I'll make sure that it hurts. Understand?"

Kurt tried to loosen my grip. He was a good 4 inches taller and a whole lot heavier, but I had the power of absolute fury at the moment. Finally, he understood his position and nodded.

I let go. Kurt took a gulp of air and yanked at his collar. There was a faint red mark on his throat.

"Don't come anywhere near me the rest of the day," I said quietly.

He nodded again, rubbing his throat. In the doorway, though, he paused, looking at Heather and Troy.

"We didn't see a thing," Troy told him. "Did we, Heather?"

"Actually," she said, "I wasn't even here. I imagine it's just another rumor."

Kurt left, still rubbing his throat.

"You'd better watch it, Dev," Troy said as soon as the coast was clear again. "All hell's going to break loose with him sometime. Maybe you'd better get a sex life, just to be safe." Heather elbowed him, hard. "Hey! That hurt!"

"Thanks," I told her. "Now, what color did we decide on for the banner?"

☙☘

Troy was right, although not about the source of all the hell that broke loose. That happened that very night, when Cassie walked in on Monica and me.

The shock couldn't have been greater had Jerry Falwell walked in wearing a dress. I fell out of bed—an event precipitated largely by the fact that the part I'd been lying on was gone. The enormous bed had simply vanished when Cassie opened the door, along with the rest of the vampire trappings, and I was lying on very solid real-world carpet. Fortunately, I still had my real-world robe on. Cassie, for her part, had backed up against the wall so hard that it constituted a nasty vertical fall.

"Oh, my God," she was saying. "I didn't mean to . . . I mean, I didn't know . . ."

I scrambled to my feet and looked around with an eye to damage control. The situation seemed to call for all kinds of control. There was the situation itself, for one thing. Also, I was bleeding, thanks to one of Monica's sharp parts. Then, of course, there was Monica herself. She was propped up against the headboard, totally unclothed, totally unconcerned. When I looked at her, she just smiled and patted the place in bed beside her invitingly.

Pretending not to understand, I turned from her to Cassie, who was starting to get a little color back. Her eyes, though, were still the size of CDs.

"I'm sorry," she said, barely audibly. "I wasn't thinking. But I didn't expect—"

"Never mind that right now. How'd you get in?"

She held up the spare key.

"But I moved it a couple of months ago."

Cassie shrugged, as if to say that even a Chihuahua could outwit me, and dropped the key on the dresser. She still hadn't looked at me directly.

"Would it be too trite to ask what you're doing here?" I asked.

"I heard what happened with Kurt today. I wanted to see if you were all right. You must not be—you didn't actually kill him."

I let that go. "You could have rung the doorbell, at least."

"Where's the fun in that?" A faint smile and eye contact, finally. "No, really, I *did* ring this time. You didn't answer. I got worried. But if everything's all right . . ."

"Oh, yes," Monica assured her. "Perfectly all right. As you see." She turned to me, smiled, and patted the bed again.

Cassie's smile vanished, and I didn't like the look that replaced it. Unsure what to do, I tried acting normal. "Maybe I should introduce the two of you. Monica, Cassie. Cassie, Mon—"

"She's the woman I saw you with at that party," Cassie said suddenly.

That didn't register right away. "What?"

"Greg and Linda's party. She's the woman I saw you with that night." Cassie's tone was flat. "The one you wouldn't tell me about."

She was studying Monica, who remained calm and even amused by the scrutiny. Something hostile seemed to meet between them, and lock.

Stop it. You're already imagining too many things.

To Cassie, I said, "Right. You're right. Great memory. Listen, there's something I need to tell you about. You see—"

Monica hooked a fingernail under the sash of my robe. "Not yet, baby duck. Remember your manners. Offer our guest a drink."

Wincing, I hoped against hope that Cassie hadn't heard that. Unfortunately . . .

" 'Baby duck'?" Cassie repeated, incredulous. "Lady, that's *my* line. Where do you get off—"

I cut her off. She didn't know who, or what, she was about to insult. "Never mind. She's right. Manners are good. Let's have manners. May I offer you a drink?"

"Baby duck?" Cassie asked Monica again, ignoring me.

"I'm having a brandy myself. But if you'd rather—"

"Baby duck," Monica confirmed. "May I ask why you object when you call her so much worse?"

"Excuse me?"

They were almost the whole room apart, but just to be safe, I stepped between them. "Maybe you should leave, Cass. We can talk about this tomorrow."

If they heard, they gave no sign.

"Let me refresh your memory," Monica told Cassie. "Pornographer. Pervert. Deviant. Caligula—and various parts of his tribune. Does any of this sound familiar?"

"You left out Antichrist," Cassie said coolly. "What are you? A spy?"

"After a fashion. I'm her demon."

"Her what?"

"Shall I spell it? D-e-m—"

Cassie glared at her and then wheeled on me. "This isn't funny, Devvy."

"I know. You'd better go."

"Yes," Monica said, taking a firmer hold on my sash. "We can do without venial bitches after hours. Can't we?"

Demon or not, she'd just gone one round too many. I pushed her hand away in a fit of temper, not knowing—or really caring—what the consequences would be. "Damn you, Monica, back off her. You can't talk to her like that. I don't care if you're the Beast of Revelation—you can't . . ."

I broke off, startled by the slam of the front door. Cassie was gone.

"Was it something I said?" Monica asked sweetly.

CHAPTER 10
THE MORNING AFTER

Three times from nine to nine-thirty the next morning, I walked down to Cassie's office and knocked. Three times, she didn't answer. But she was in there, all right, along with Heart.

All right, technically, just "If Looks Could Kill."

"She's been playing it since I got here," an admin reported wearily, "and I was early today. Who'd she go out with last night?"

Finally, I did in the last place what I should've done in the first place: went across the street to the phone booth on the corner. Outside calls rang in differently. I knew she'd pick up.

"This is Cassandra Wolfe of J/J/G Advertising. I'm away from my office. But if you'll leave a brief mes—"

"Knock it off, Cass," I told her. "I can hear the music. Can we talk?"

"—short message after the beep, I'll return your call as soon as—"

"We can yell, if you'd rather. You can do all the yelling. But we really need to—"

"Beep," Cassie said, and hung up.

Momentarily bewildered, I hung up too—and then grabbed the receiver and hung up again so hard that the whole phone booth shuddered. A passing yup in a Volvo slowed to give me a disapproving once-over. For his benefit, I did it again.

Then I stormed back across the street and up the stairs two at a time, dead-heating with Cassie at my office door.

"I take it back, Cass. Now *I* want to do all the yelling."

"We'll take turns. I'll go first."

"I go first. It's my office."

"True," she said, holding up a bakery bag, "but these are my chocolate-chip muffins."

I glared at her, at the bag, at her, and then threw open the office door.

Cassie poured herself a mug of my private coffee while I took one of her muffins. Chocolate-chip, all right, with chocolate icing. Maybe she wasn't so mad after all.

"I could cheerfully kill you," she said.

All right, so maybe she was. "And God forbid you be *un*cheerful about it. That could get you talked about. The rude murderess. The uncivil—"

"I could cheerfully kill you, and no jury in the world would give me more than community service. But any judge who'd ever met you would just pardon me anyway, on the grounds that killing you *was* community service. Do you have any idea what you put me through last night?"

"Cass, you're going to tell me whether I ask or not, so—"

"You could have told me, you know. Should have told me. I shouldn't have had to find out like that. I'm a grown woman, and I've had cable TV for ages. You should've told me. I would've been very mature about it."

I snorted and tossed the rest of my muffin into the wastebasket.

"I beg your pardon?" she asked frostily.

"Quit telling lies. You'd have done just what you did last night, only sooner. You always said you'd hate to see what would go out with me, and now I see that you meant every word of it."

"Don't change the subject. I'm not done with you about the

surprise aspect of all this. But now that we're talking about the witch . . ."

"Just because you don't like her is no reason to call her names. I don't like most of the birth-control accidents you go out with, either, but at least I don't say so."

Coolly, Cassie emptied her coffee into my wastebasket and then threw the mug in, too, for good measure.

"That's *your* mug, Cass."

"Fine. Let me see yours for a minute."

I snatched it out of her reach just in time. "You're overreacting."

"And you're not?"

"It's not like I thought this up, you know. Sex has been around for years. Besides, *she* came after *me*."

"She should've used a bigger gun. Then she could've blown you into a million pieces, and I could've worn a great black dress to the funeral."

I was already starting to lose my temper, and that didn't help. "I'm dead, and all you care about is what you're wearing?"

"Your funeral," she informed me, "will be a black-tie social occasion. People are going to come from every continent, just to make sure you're really extinct. I'll want to look my best."

"Thank God I'll be dead," I grumbled.

"Oh, you'll be dead, all right. A dead hypocrite. Not even just a hypocrite—a fool on top of it. Do you think she loves you?"

It had never occurred to me to wonder. "Does it matter?"

"You're such an idiot. *Yes*, it matters. First time in years—you probably think she invented sex—and you think it means she loves you, even though *normal* people don't bite, even though *normal* people don't—"

"Coming from you, Cass," I said, with edge, "this is flat-out jabberwocky. Tell me what love has to do with *your* love life.

You go through men like they're Pez. No, don't tell me; that's different; they're men. But let *me* happen to hook up with a woman—*one* woman—and you act like—"

"She owes her womanhood to science, if you ask me. Get your eyes checked. You know what else you're too stupid to see? *She doesn't love you.*"

Furious, I swept the bakery bag off the desk into the wastebasket. Then I shouldered her aside, none too gently, en route to the door.

Cassie jumped back in front of me. "Don't you dare walk. I'm not through. And you know I'm right."

"Move," I told her dangerously, "or be moved."

"By you and what five hundred Brownie Scouts?"

All right. Fine. She'd asked for it. I backtracked to the wastebasket, picked it up, and did a quick inventory. Coffee, muffins, wadded-up paper, some dead gum, Cassie's fancy china mug. Good.

"What are you doing?"

"Think fast," I advised her, and turned the wastebasket upside down on her head.

She shrieked something about hairdressers and dry cleaning and death, but I couldn't make it all out, what with that wastebasket on her head. Game, set, and match to Kerry. I made a point of slamming the office door behind me.

Halfway down the hall, I heard the door slam open again, followed by the loud clear information that Cassie hated me and wanted something big and heavy to run over me a couple hundred times. I kept walking.

"What is it this time?" Heather asked in passing.

"She doesn't like the woman I'm sleeping with."

"Oh, stop it, Dev. What is it really?"

I kept walking.

Chapter II
A Couple Days Later

The next two days were deceptively quiet. Through interoffice mail, I'd sent Cassie a check for what I figured was twice the damage, and she'd e-mailed to say that she'd cashed it right away, before I could change my weasel mind. We'd had no other contact, though, which was probably wise.

Still, we had to work together. In fact, we had an appointment with a client on Thursday, so we'd have to work together in public. I planned to stop by her office before the appointment to try to break the ice.

She'd saved me the trouble, though. That morning, I found a note in Cassie's angular handwriting taped to my office door:

> *We have that 3:00 with the paintball people. There.*
> *I'm driving.*
> *P.S.: I still hate you.*

Great. She was finally coming around.

☙

We got to The Hot Zone about two seconds after we left J/J/G. Cassie drove too fast even when she wasn't upset, and when she was, she was lightning. That was fine with me, though, because getting there early gave us time to look around on our own. Who knew what the client wouldn't want us to see?

The first thing we saw was that there wasn't a customer in the place. True, it was the middle of a weekday afternoon, but a few years ago, you couldn't get in even then for love or money. Fads came late to Meridian and died there early. No wonder the owner wanted an ad agency.

"Smoke machines," I ventured, pushing open the double doors to peer into the dark playing field. "Smoke machines, follow spots, and models in Mazola and floss. We'll do it like a coed *Heart of Darkness*. What do you think?"

Cassie, who'd said nothing since we'd left the office, continued to say nothing. Pointedly, she turned away to study the price board.

Just then, a sallow young man with a ponytail emerged through the door behind the ticket desk. "You the ones from the ad agency? Boss'll be right out."

Cassie didn't even glance at the clerk when she spoke to him. She was still absorbed in the price board. "Is that the price for an hour?"

"Yeah. But you get your uniforms and your guns and stuff for that. You gotta give us a deposit, but it ain't bad. We give it back."

"Suppose that my colleague and I want to play. For, say, two hours. How much?"

"I dunno. It's usually just an hour."

"What if we want extra cartridges? How much for those?"

The conversation no longer sounded like research. I let the doors to the playing field swing shut and rushed over to set things straight. "We're not here to play," I told the clerk. "We're just here to look the place over. To get some ideas for the ad cam—"

"Two hours," Cassie told the clerk. She started rummaging through her attaché. "A hundred rounds apiece to start. Do you take platinum AmEx?"

"She's kidding," I assured him. Then, to her: "You're kidding. Paintball? Us?"

"Us. Right now." She slapped a card down on the counter and resumed her directions to the clerk. "I won't make you do the math. Ring it up as two separate hours, if you have to. We'll take the same size in uniforms, except mine will need *much* more room in the chest. What about shoes?"

I covered the card with my hand. "We're not playing."

"We're playing," she told the clerk. "Do you take titanium Visa?"

The manager appeared in time to see Cassie marching off to the locker room with her gear. I explained the situation to him while the clerk piled my equipment on the counter.

"But you don't have to pay," the manager protested. "Jeff, don't charge them. This is business."

"Let her pay," I said grimly. "And give me the very best gun you've got."

CB&SO

Had the Jedi looked even half as silly as I did, *Star Wars* would never have made popcorn money. It wasn't just that the uniform didn't fit very well, or that the boots and gloves didn't go with it, or even that the helmet was stupid. It was that I looked about ten years old, dressed up in my daddy's old Army clothes to go play war in the back yard. I'd never done that when I *was* ten, or at any other time. Now I was never mind how much more older, and this was stupid to the last power. What was Cassie's damage? Only teenage dweebs and chipheads played paintball nowadays. Besides, violence was so damn . . .

Macho.

Scowling at my reflection in the mirror, I flipped the visor down and then went upstairs to find my opponent.

She was already on the playing field, checking her weapon. *She* didn't look silly, much less macho. She looked terrific and extremely female—not to mention dangerous as hell.

"Didn't I see you in *The Quick and the Dead*?" I asked.

Cassie ignored that entirely. "The rules are that there are no rules. We can kill each other as many times as we want. Then we can go back and get more cartridges. Start the timer."

"Not so fast. Let's agree on one thing first: We don't have to do this for two whole hours. OK? If it's no fun, we—"

"It'll be fun. I'm going to enjoy this. Start the timer."

I found the timer button on the wall and poised a finger over it. She stepped to the start line, gun drawn, and put her visor down. We eyed each other suspiciously.

"Do paintballs hurt?" I wondered.

"I hope so. Start the timer."

Just before I actually pushed the button, though, Cassie aimed, fired—and hit.

I jumped, stung. "Hey!"

She fired again, with equal success. Then she sprinted off into the dark.

I rubbed my shoulder—paintballs *did* hurt, as it turned out—and punched the timer button, vowing to make the cheater taste paint. Two could play this stupid chiphead game.

⋘⋙

A couple of hundred cartridges later, we called it quits. We were both every color by then, and by all appearances, she wasn't mad at me anymore. I figured that she'd finally killed me enough times to have gotten it out of her system. Even if she hadn't, I was too tired to kill her back anymore.

We showered and changed, thanked the manager, and went off to the Pig & Whistle to observe truce. I bought.

"To peace," I proposed. "Such as you ever give me."

"To the worst friend I ever had."

"Or the best enemy."

"Same difference."

We drank to that.

"What did you do with the mushrooms?" she asked.

I searched the table, shifting baskets: mozzarella sticks, onion chips, chicken fingers, eggrolls, nachos, baby ribs. Our plan was to have a light snack here and order a couple of pizzas at her place later, after we ordered some pay-per-view. Eventually, I found the mushrooms backed up against the wall of the booth behind the salsa and the Chinese mustard.

"Trade you the potato skins," Cassie said.

We rearranged baskets. Just then, a man in an overly tailored suit cleared his throat over my shoulder.

"Afternoon," he told Cassie. "Leo Carter. Carter Realty. I see that you're alone. I just ordered you a bottle of much better wine than that. How can you possibly thank me?"

I mentally rescheduled my evening. Tall, attractive, obnoxious, breathing—he was her type, all right.

To my surprise, though, she declined, and rather tartly at that.

Her suitor was surprised, too. He persisted. She refused him again, in a tone that meant business.

"Look at the time," I said to no one in particular. "I should be going. Thanks for the—"

She reached over the table to grab my arm. "We just got here, I drove, and I'm not ready to leave yet."

"I have my Land Rover," he told her. "What if we call your friend a cab? You're too pretty to waste your evening."

Cassie's eyes went ballistic blue—and I knew all too well what that meant. Briefly, I considered diving under the table for cover. But it was too late. By the time she finally stopped to draw a breath, Leo Carter, Carter Realty, was halfway to his Land Rover, almost running out of range of her terrible voice.

There was a brief, shocked silence in the bar. Then all the other women there—every last one of them—broke into applause.

Cassie raised her glass to them and then turned back to me. My jaw was still on the floor.

"A woman's prerogative," she said triumphantly. "Have a cheese stick."

ᘓᘒᘓ

A few minutes after midnight, I watched the taillights of Cassie's BMW turn the corner and then walked into the condo, braced for the worst. I had a very bad feeling that I should have called Monica to say I'd be late—but it wasn't like I had her phone number, right? Besides, I had every right to spend an evening with a friend. Monica didn't own me. She was just my demon, not—

All right, maybe she *did* own me. There might be hell to pay for this, and it was probably time to make a payment. Might as well get it over with. "Monica?"

No answer. A faint light, however, was flickering in the upstairs hallway. I went up to investigate. The door of the master bath was ajar. I pushed it open to find Monica taking a bubble bath by candlelight.

"So," she said, "you played a nice little chiphead game. And she agreed to keep me a secret. To protect you."

"She did. But how did you—?"

"You still have paint in your hair. Shall I lather you up?"

"What paint? I took a shower."

"Stop being so literal. You lose all the romance that way. Join me."

I studied her, wary. Her eyes were glittering, but no fangs were visible, and she seemed to be in a good mood, for her. Still, there was something a little too avid about her. Being ready for a quick getaway might not be a bad idea. So I took off only my watch and shoes, and got into the tub.

Monica laughed and drew me close, her fingernails pointed lightly against my throat like the caress of razor wire. Then, with her free hand, she reached for the soap and rubbed my cheek with it.

"More paint? But I took a—"

"No. Not paint." She massaged the soap in with her fingertips.

Then I remembered. "Oh. That? It was nothing. Just good night."

"Was it?"

"Ask her yourself, if you don't believe me."

Monica began to use her fingernails, not hard, but not gently either. "I don't believe that I will. She doesn't like me much, does she?"

"Wonder why," I said dryly. "Considering that you went out of your way to insult her."

"While we're wondering things, I wonder why she kissed you at all."

"She had a little too much wine." I winced. Monica was beginning to scratch, and she might have drawn blood. "Shouldn't that be off by now?"

"Shouldn't you be tempted by now?"

"I don't know what you're talking about."

"You will," Monica said. Then she started to lick the cut in my cheek.

CHAPTER 12
AFTER THAT

Cassie was as good as her word. She didn't say a thing to anyone about Monica, and it must have killed her, but she kept quiet. That worked. I was paranoid about anyone's finding out, and she approved of the paranoia, and even encouraged it. She lied and weaseled around the truth, when necessary, to help protect me—which, after all, is what friends are for but which was still good of her.

Moreover, she was careful not to talk about Monica even to me. Once in a while, I would forget and say her name, and Cassie would bristle. I was grateful for the reminder and would make a point of trying not to slip up again.

She was a brick, all right. Take the way she handled the social situation.

I'd had to stop going to J/J/G parties because of Monica. I wasn't about to take a date—much less a female date—to one of those things. Accordingly, I'd been missing a couple of social occasions a week for a while, and some people were starting to take it personally. After all, I'd never been picky before. I'd even gone to a party that Randy Harris threw once. One day, Walt cornered me after a meeting and demanded to know why I wouldn't be at his party that night.

Cassie didn't miss a beat. "She just got a cat."

"A cat?" Walt asked, not following—which made two of us.

"A big black cat. With a very bad temper. It's had *lots* of surgery."

I started to protest, but Cassie stared me into silence.

"So?" Walt asked.

"It doesn't like to be left alone at night. Or so I hear."

"Hell, Dev, you can bring the cat," Walt said. "Sparky might chase it a little, but—"

Cassie shook her head. "Not a good idea. This animal is vicious. It bites."

He looked me over thoughtfully. "Oh. Well, then, that would explain it."

There was no need to ask what it explained. I'd been using a lot of Bactine lately.

"Besides," Cassie added, "you wouldn't like her. The cat, I mean. I think Devvy's afraid of her. Did I tell you she sleeps on the bed?"

"Sounds a little kinky to me."

"You have no idea," she said wearily.

Walt laughed. "You're awfully quiet, Dev. Cat got your tongue?"

He found this question *trés amusant*, and Cassie pretended to, just to spite me. There being no point in taking offense, I simply walked away. Why fight the inevitable? There'd be cat jokes the rest of the day now, no matter what. Shortly after I got back to my office, e-mail came through:

> Just CATastrophic that you CAn'T make the party. Hope your little critter will be FELINE better soon. CATch you next time? Sure would be MICE to see you.

I trashed it and got back to work.

⟷

All that aside, though, I was starting to have some hope that everything might be all right. I had Cassie's help and Monica's promise—whatever it was worth—and all three of us were professional liars, in our ways. This situation might not be too much for three pros to manage.

If I could only keep going the way I'd always done before, maybe it would all work out. With luck, I could have Monica, my job, and my secret too.

Hope never hurt anyone, right?

❧

The Monday when everything started going wrong started with two hours in a small conference room with Jack, Kurt, Heather, and Troy, trying to come up with a campaign for a hair salon. Whether it was because of Monday or because of some marital unpleasantness, Kurt was worse than usual. He'd started three arguments in the first half-hour, and he'd only been warming up.

Jack liked to say that my team would be in jail in any decent, civilized country, but he was just smart enough to let my writers go only so far. That day, however, he was giving Kurt way too much leash. Kurt was in a mood, and he wanted raw sex on the screen. Failing that, he wanted busty models in thongs and spike heels. He also wanted the models.

We had all tried to rein him in—all except Jack, who was playing Buddha, saying nothing. Finally, when Kurt proposed cleavage cam, Heather lost it.

"You stupid jerkoff pig, you don't even know what you're talking about."

"I know my cleavage," Kurt said with dignity.

"The client, you ass. You don't know Thing One about the client. Didn't you read the research? What's the market? Who's the audience?"

"What's it matter? This is a proven sales tech—"

"*Women*, Kurt. Look." She waved a research report in his face. "Right here. See? Says that eighty-seven percent of the client's customers are *women*."

"So?"

Heather, baffled, looked to me for help. Of course, I had none to offer.

"OK, so we'll give the ladies something too. We'll pose a couple of guys in the background and take their shirts off," Kurt said. "Give them scissors, but make 'em not look like hairdressers."

Heather frowned. "What does *that* mean?"

"Make 'em look straight."

"You really are a pig. Are all men who cut hair gay?"

"Aren't all male models?"

Now Troy was upset too. Jack just beamed at me. He was basking in the nasty vibe in the room and clearly wasn't going to intervene.

All right, fine—up to me again. I gave Kurt a very bad look. "I half-expected you to say we should shoot the thing on a Thursday and have the male models wear green. Are you still in junior high, boy? Get a grip. This isn't about sexual orientation."

"Says you," he shot back. "Who wrote 'Tempted?', boss?"

Bull's-eye. I withdrew from the field, bloodied, bowed, and guilty as charged.

Jack laughed—the first sound he'd made since he called the meeting to order. "I live for meets with this team. You people ought to be in rehab. Let's massage this idea a little and see what comes up. What's your last shot, Wheeler?"

Kurt drew rapidly on his notepad and pushed it across the table. "I'm no artist—"

"No shit," grumbled Troy, leaning over to see.

"—but this pretty much blocks it out for you."

I took a look too, unfortunately. The sketch was a tight shot of a seated stick-figure man, with very large breasts appearing to grow out of his ears.

"Don't know, Wheeler," Jack mused. "People'll think the hooters come with the haircuts."

"Exactly," Kurt said.

Heather and Troy protested, to no avail. I closed my eyes and hoped Monica would put me out of my misery for good that night.

⋘⋙

The meeting finally broke up a few minutes before noon with nothing resolved, as usual, so we'd essentially wasted the morning, as usual. Hadn't this business been fun once? I was on my way to my office for several Advil when Heather caught up.

"You look a little peaked, Dev. Want to go to lunch? Get some fresh air?"

"No Kurt?"

"Absolutely no Kurt. We want to talk about him, don't we?"

I agreed, on condition that everything we said about him would be bad. That, she said, was the whole idea. We decided to walk the few blocks to the restaurant, to make the talk last longer.

Heather was right about the benefits of fresh air and invective. By the time we were a block down Virginia, I was feeling better.

"I don't understand why you won't ever let me kill him," Heather was saying.

"Peg has first right. By marriage."

"I can't imagine why she married him."

"Can't be because of his charm."

"You don't suppose . . . ?" She considered. "Naaah. I'll bet he still wears little boys' underpants. With Spider-Man on them."

"*There's* a theory. I don't like to picture it, but it's a theory." I smiled at her. "So you're saying all this talk of his is just overcompensation?"

"Well, why not? You know about Henry VIII's codpiece, don't you?"

I'd seen the pictures. She had a point. "Every man would have a codpiece like that if men still wore armor. They're all as vain as show dogs. But Kurt would overdo *that*. He'd have a codpiece that'd make Henry's look like an anchovy."

"Well, there's a saying about that. There's a Spanish proverb: 'If you can't fight, wear a big hat.'"

I had to stop and lean against a lamppost to laugh.

"Seriously," Heather assured me.

"Maybe we should get him a sombrero."

"Of course, I notice that you wear a hat sometimes," she said slyly.

"It goes with my raincoat." True. I had a fabulous long black raincoat and a black fedora to match. The first time I'd worn them together, Cassie had said, "No, don't tell me; let me guess. Boris Badenov?" Ever since, to spite her, I often wore both coat and hat whenever it even just might rain.

Heather just smiled.

"Don't start," I told her.

"I'm not starting. I'm just noticing. I think it looks perfectly adorable on you, if you like that sort of—" She broke off, squinting across the street. "Hey, isn't that Jenner? With the Hardware City girl?"

It was Jenner, all right, going into a restaurant with a very young woman in a dress of a type that wasn't designed to be worn before five. The last time I'd seen her, she was fondling a snowblower on a billboard, wearing only fur and enough lip gloss to choke a pig. A rival agency handled the account, which was fine by me.

I wondered whether Heather knew that the Hardware City

girl was also sleeping with Jack, with Stu Bennett at Ad House, and with a cast of maybe thousands more. But she didn't have to know that yet. She was still young, and she still thought this business was fun.

"Sleeping with the enemy," I remarked, nodding at the spectacle across the street.

"Don't we all?"

Some of us more than others, I thought.

"I mean, those of us who sleep with people," Heather amended.

"Well, that leaves out Peg."

Heather laughed, as though it were a joke.

☙❧

After lunch, I went straight to my office and closed the door, hoping not to have to deal with anyone for the rest of the day. But the moment I turned, I got a very bad surprise.

She was curled up in my chair, completely at home—and apparently unharmed by sunlight, which was flooding that end of the office. So much for that myth.

"What are you doing here?" I whispered. "You promised not to—"

"You had a hard morning," Monica said. "I thought I'd come cheer you up."

"Not at the office, you won't. Did anyone see you?"

"No one saw me. Your secret is safe. For now."

"For now?" I turned that over a few times and then frowned. "Wait a minute. Cassie can see you. Always *has* seen you. How do I know you're not lying about—"

"You need a haircut. I hear that they come with lady parts at some salons."

"You hear wrong. Don't try to throw me off track here, Monica. This is important. What do you mean by 'for now'?"

Monica left my chair. "Sit."

It wasn't a request; it was an order. So I sat. She crossed behind the chair and pressed up against me, all the way—exactly like Kurt's sketch, in fact. "What are you doing?"

"Research. I want to see whether that shot will work. What do you think?"

"What if someone comes in?"

"You're about to find out," she said calmly as the door opened.

Kurt. I felt all the blood drain out of my head. Of all the people to catch me in a compromising position . . .

"What's wrong, boss? You look kind of rattled."

Monica pressed even closer—and I realized then that he didn't see her. She'd told the truth. For now. The relief wasn't as great as it might have been, though.

"You're fired the next time you don't knock first," I warned him. "What do you want?"

"Just wanted to give you the first draft on Hairport."

"Inbox."

He looked curiously at me and dropped the script in the box. "You sure you're OK?"

"Fine."

"I took out that shot."

"Fine. If that's all, get out."

"That's all." Reluctantly, he made for the door, and then turned back at the threshold. "I really advise you to get laid, boss. This can't be worth it."

"*Out!*"

Monica laughed—and as soon as the door closed behind Kurt, I started to order her out, too. But I was ordering empty air. She was gone.

This couldn't be good. J/J/G wasn't going to be big enough for all of us—and her. We already had enough devils. We didn't need a demon.

Chapter 13
October

October, Monica said, is the witching month, and anything can happen. Like I needed her to tell me that. What with Christmas campaigns winding down, spring campaigns gearing up, and the agency's Halloween party looming at the end, October was always a nightmare.

So it was no real surprise that the nightmare started right on schedule. The very first meeting of the month was with Tom of Tom's Country Catering, who wanted a Christmas promotion, and it started badly even for a client meeting. Tom wanted to be in the ads. He wanted to help write the copy. He wanted to dress up like Santa and possibly pose with reindeer. Cassie and Chip were pouring tact over him like maple syrup, trying to persuade him that all that detail work would be undignified for a man of his stature, but he wasn't budging. Bored, I wished that they would tell him the truth about clients' ideas or just resign the account so that I wouldn't have to listen to this argument for the millionth time. Besides, the man's size was all the advertising his business really needed anyway.

To be polite, I focused on the client before tuning out for what I hoped would be a nice rest. But then something went wrong with my vision. One minute, a fat man was sitting in the client's chair, and the next, Monica was . . . fingering the top button of her gown and giving me her most incendiary smile.

I knew what it meant—and knew even better that this wasn't the time or place. I tried to look away but wound up looking down anyway and then couldn't quite look away again. Literally couldn't—it was like my focus was locked.

"You're staring at my tie," Monica purred.

Tie? I blinked . . . and the client was back in that chair, looking aggrieved. "She's staring at my tie," he told Jack.

Cassie, sitting directly across the table from me, looked up from her research report to study me narrowly. What could I say? Fortunately, Jack thought of something first.

"She's just like a parakeet," he told the client, all charm. "Gets fascinated by bright shiny objects. We have to keep her completely away from Christmas trees so she won't hurt herself."

The client's tie *was* a bright shiny object—a hideous hot-yellow satin thing—but I resented the parakeet part all to hell. And Jack knew it. He was grinning at me in his nastiest way. I was about to ask him to step outside so I could kill him in private when Troy jumped in.

"You know, that color might work really well as the signature color for the campaign," he told the client. "Red and green get done to death at Christmas, and yellow is a good food-related color. What do you think?"

The client didn't know what to think but started talking anyway, and the crisis was over.

"Thanks," I whispered to Troy, who winked back.

I willed myself to pay attention and not zone out anymore. But the client had one of those half-track minds, so he got right back to the Santa concept. Cassie and Chip went back to work on him, and in self-defense, I went AWOL again.

Monica had a half-track mind in some ways, too. When she materialized again, her gown was mostly open, and she was wearing the ruby crucifix down where I knew I couldn't look in public. She began to tug the chain up and down, slowly, so that the cross rode up and down her cleavage, very slowly, up and down, up and down, up and d—

"Now she's staring at *his* tie," the client complained.

I found myself focused on Chip, who was trying not to laugh.

"Must be his tie tack," Jack told the client happily.

Cassie gave him a look that could have cut glass. "We don't want to embarrass her by calling attention to her problem, do we, Jack?" Then, to the client: "Please don't take offense. Devvy doesn't always know what she's doing. She was in a car crash a couple of months ago and hit her head."

I resented that, too, but Cassie had just kicked me under the table—a little harder than necessary. By the look in her eye, she wasn't sure what was going on but wasn't taking any chances.

"Oh," the client said, visibly relieved. "Yeah, sure. I see now. I had a cousin that happened to once."

"Was he ever right again?" Jack asked innocently. "If you don't mind my asking."

"Oh, sure. After a couple months. Well, more like three."

Jack leaned back, positively sated. "Then there you have it. We'll have Kerry back in time to stuff the Thanksgiving turkey. Isn't that great news?"

What with one thing and another, the meeting was clearly no longer safe, so I pushed my chair back and stood. "Forgive me for the distractions, Mr. Johnson. My writers can help you on creative for the rest of the meeting. I'm going to lie down for a while."

"You don't want to fool with a head injury," the client agreed.

With as much dignity as possible, and making sure not to let Kurt catch my eye, I left the conference room. A few steps down the hallway, I heard the client say, "Could take longer than three months. My cousin spent about that long just watching the shopping channel, day and night."

I decided to *really* go lie down.

❧

An hour or so later, Kurt popped his head into my office. "Feeling better now, Tweety?"

"You'd better be here to give me a report on the Tom's meeting. Then you'd better be gone."

"I'll type up my notes and shoot 'em to you on e-mail, if you want."

"I want. Now go."

"One more thing, boss. Real fast. Got a second?"

I saved the file and leaned back, arms crossed, looking as ominous as possible.

"I was really taken with the way you looked at Chip's tie tack," he said. "There was something almost . . . sexual about it. Can you show me just one more time how you did it?"

I got up and moved toward him with intent.

"Just for research. I might use it in an ad."

I kept walking.

"OK," Kurt said quickly, and got out of the room a step ahead of bodily harm.

Jerk. But a very observant jerk. I'd have to think of something to do about him if Monica was going to be like this for long.

❧

That night when I got home, she was stretched out in front of the fireplace like a cat, naked.

"Someday, you're going to shock me," I told her.

"Very jaded for a former celibate."

"You may have had a little to do with that." Sighing, I threw my coat and attaché in the nearest chair. She might be ready to go for a spin, but I couldn't shift gears quite that fast. "Do I have time for a drink?"

Monica pointed to the hearth, where two brandies were warming. Careful not to step on her, I picked up the snifters, handed one down, and started toward the couch.

"You'll be more comfortable here with me," she said. "Please. Get comfortable."

That was all the way out of character, and it threw me for a second. "You're not going to just pounce? Or scratch? Or bite?"

"You don't trust me."

"No."

"Try. Or I *will* pounce and scratch and bite."

Well, then, what did I have to lose? Carefully, I lay down next to her. She reached over. I braced against pain—and felt only a gentle touch.

My shock must have shown, because she explained herself. "You've had a hard day. Again. You've had a hard year, actually. Six hard years. Have you finally had enough tough love?"

Startled, I laughed. "Tough what?"

"Tough love. You don't seem to be acquainted with any other kind."

"I'm not really acquainted with any kind. But don't you mean tough sex?"

"If you wouldn't fight me, it wouldn't have to be."

"I don't fight you."

"You do mentally. You just think I don't know it." She smoothed my hair. "You can actually be rather sweet when you forget how evil I am."

"Well," I said reluctantly, "you have your moments too."

"Imagine the damage to my reputation if that got out."

"*Your* reputation? What about mine? I wouldn't last ten minutes in this town if this got out."

"You wouldn't last ten minutes at your agency, you mean. Such a vicious place. Such sharp tongues, and so much talk."

She continued to stroke my hair. "When you come home at night, I can smell the fear on you for an hour."

"That's not fear. It's Jack's cigars." I grimaced. "Ever since I quit smoking, I can't stand the smell of smoke, even on people's clothes. Can you imagine how *I* must've smelled? Two packs a day, and—what?"

She had leaned into me and was sniffing delicately. "Ahhh. Eau de Fear. Really, the Bulgari works better on you, but there's no accounting for your taste."

"You sound like Cassie sometimes," I grumbled.

"Imagine that. Now, where were we before you changed the subject in such a hurry? Oh, yes. We were talking about all the talk at your office."

"I don't want to talk about it."

"Of course not. You've had a long day. You're tired." She kissed my forehead and worked her way down softly, almost lovingly.

Grateful, I pulled her closer. "Like I said, you have your moments."

She paused. "Oh. That's right. I almost forgot. I'm evil." Then, before I could react, she pushed me down and bit.

CHAPTER 14
STILL OCTOBER

Then there was Rumours, the Rasputin of accounts.

For two months, I'd been editing, recutting, and generally power-tweaking the "Tempted?" spot, trying to find a balance between what the clients wanted and what the lawyers would allow. On those rare occasions when the work met both sides' approval, it hadn't met Jenner's. I suspected that Jack was behind all the bother, just to make my life as complicated as possible—as though I needed *him* for that.

Finally, though, the damn thing was done—and ironically, it wasn't much different from the original. The only content change was the kiss in the middle, which had been reshot with a clearly heterosexual couple. I'd also had to recut the segment with the unconventional pairings. They were all still there, but now, some of them were flashed on the screen as subliminal images. I'd fought Jenner and Jack about that for a month, but it was like trying to reason with the lords of the Late Roman Empire. This ad was just what their home movies might've been, if only they'd had the camcorders.

The ad was finally done, though, and finally out of my hands. By now, I was sick of the spot, sorry that I'd written it, and ready to get the final in-house screening over so that I'd never have to see it again. That was how I always felt about my ads by the time they went out, but this one was especially unbearable now.

My co-workers, however, had a much higher threshold of pain. When I got to the conference room, a few minutes early, they were already there, running the tape.

"Jenner and Jack aren't here yet," I pointed out.

No one paid any attention. So I just took a chair and looked out the window, trying not to even hear the music. I was sick of that by now, too.

When it was over, there was heavy silence.

"Somebody give me a cigarette," Walt finally said.

"You don't smoke," Chip reminded him.

"I'm smoking right now. That's why I need the cigarette." Nervous laughter, mercifully interrupted by the arrival of Jenner and Jack.

"I'll see it," Jenner said, taking his chair.

Jack ran the video. At the end, to everyone's astonishment, Jenner started laughing.

"Sir?" Jack asked.

"This'll just kill that sonuvabitch Bennett at Ad House. Thinks he can outdeviant me, does he? Not in *my* town. Fine work, Miss Devlin. I ought to promote you one of these days."

I guessed that the man was off his medication again, so I said nothing.

"It's just a small account," Jack said stiffly. "Late-night cable and a little print, in the underground tabs."

"But people will talk, Harper. We *want* talk. Talk is good for business." Jenner reached into an inside suit pocket for a microcassette recorder and clicked it on. "Miss Sanchez, mail a cassette of the 'Tempted?' spot to the Family Foundation. Anonymous. No label on the tape. Plain mailer; postage stamps. Mail it from another zip code, while you're at it." He turned off the recorder and grinned at Jack. "That'll get the bastards."

"Mr. Jenner, they've ignored the last three mailings. We

haven't gotten a press conference out of them since March. They might be on to us."

"This is different," Jenner told him. "There are queers in this one."

Jack considered that point. Cassie gave me a sympathetic glance, which I pretended not to see.

"I've done it again, Harper."

"Yes, sir," Jack agreed.

Jenner rose and left the room, taking the time to look down Cassie's blouse on the way out. As soon as he and Jack were safely gone, everyone exhaled.

"I should've listened to my parents and gone to nursing school," I said, mostly to myself.

An account exec I hardly knew laughed. "Yeah, you'd make a great nurse. 'You want a bedpan? Not on *my* shift. Go in your water glass.'"

"'You want a pain pill?'" Walt chimed in. "'I'll give you pain. I'll break your other leg.'"

"Sponge baths would be out of the question, of course," Kurt said, enjoying himself entirely too much.

"Well, think what you just saw," Walt said. "What if the patient's a girl?"

I froze.

"Naaah. She's celibate. That's even worse," Kurt told him. "It'd be more like this: 'You go ahead and give yourself that sponge bath, miss. I'll watch.'" Laughter.

"Knock it off, Kurt," Cassie warned.

"I can't help it," he told her happily. "I'm just naturally creative."

I got up and made for the door. "Channel it into your work for a change. I'm leaving."

"Didn't she used to be more fun?" Walt asked behind my back. Laughter.

Cassie caught up with me in the hallway. "Are you all right?"

I shrugged. "I wrote the damn ad. You tell me."

"Jenner's a squidbrain. And so are they. When did you stop knowing that?"

"When did you start defending me?" Immediately, though, I backed down. "Sorry, Cass. I guess Jenner just punched my ticket in there. I'm not big on the Q word."

"Neither am I," Cassie said, and started to add something about considering the source when we saw someone coming: Connie the Barbarian, pushing a mail cart. Both of us made all the room in the world in the hallway, and as the Barbarian passed, she tried to look down Cassie's blouse.

"Not if she were the last man on earth," Cassie growled.

"Like I said."

"Well, don't worry—you're not anything like that. At least you're perverse in your perversity."

"Just naturally creative?"

"Too much for your own good sometimes. And this is certainly one of those times. What if I talk to Sanchez and see whether I can get her to lose the tape in the mail?"

I looked at her sharply, suddenly understanding. "You've done this before, haven't you?"

"Oh, only the last three times." She smiled and patted my shoulder. "Hang in there, baby duck."

I watched her partway down the hall, then smiled too and took off in the other direction—and almost collided with the Barbarian, who was just coming out of an office.

For a split-second, I would have sworn that she winked at me. I didn't stick around long enough to find out for sure.

❧

That night, Monica wasn't there when I got home, so I took advantage of the free time to call Cassie. She answered on the last possible ring—checking Caller ID first, I figured.

"I didn't get a chance to ask later," I said, not bothering to say hello. "Did Sanchez lose the tape?"

"Tape? Tape? What tape?"

"Great. Remind me to do something nice for you sometime. But not any time soon. What are you doing home?"

"Watching a movie in bed. Alone. *That's* what I'm doing home. What are *you* doing?"

"Nothing. Monica isn't here."

"How nice of you to call to tell me that," Cassie said icily. "So you have a few free minutes before the orgy and wanted to make a pity call to your spinster friend, did you?"

"I did not. I just wanted to talk. And let's not fight on the phone. It's not as much fun."

"Oh, I don't know. It has its moments. Did I ever tell you that you sound like Daffy Duck on helium when you get really, really mad?"

I laughed. "I'm not doing this, Cass. Besides, I know better than to pity you. Considering what you usually date, a night off might be a good thing. What was the last one? A CPA?"

"That was two months ago."

"Oh. Right. So what was the last one?"

"That *was* the last one."

"Stop it. I told you, I'm not fighting with you over the—"

"Then shut up and let me tell you all about it," Cassie said.

So I shut up and let her tell me all about it. There'd been the guy who spent the whole date trying to sell her an annuity. There'd been the guy who talked bond funds with dinner and bondage with dessert. There'd been the blind date with the spray-on hair and the one with all the earrings. Then there'd been the perfect man with the fatal flaw: "He wears Old Spice. My *father* wears Old Spice."

After them was the CPA, who apparently added up short too. And that was all, she said.

"I don't believe it. St. Cassandra? Cassandra the Celibate?"

"Shut up, Devvy. You should talk."

"I know. But let me enjoy the moment."

"It isn't funny."

"I never said it was. How come you didn't tell me all this before?"

She snorted. "You think you're the only person who can have secrets?"

"No, but—"

"No, period. So stop right there."

I did. There was a long silence on the other end of the line.

"How did you stand it?" she finally asked. "Celibacy, I mean."

Oh, well, I could have at her later. So I started to tell her about long workouts, cold showers, and total abstinence from pay cable when Monica materialized in the bed and did something that made my voice crack.

"What's going on?" Cassie asked, suspicious.

"Nothing. Monica just got in. She—"

"I don't want to talk about her."

"We're not going to. Wait a minute . . . Monica? Hold that thought. I'm on the phone."

"Not anymore!" Cassie shouted, and slammed the phone down.

I listened to the dial tone for a second and then slammed the phone down myself. "Was that necessary?"

"Very," Monica said, and kept right on doing what she'd been doing.

СВЕО

The phone rang in the middle of the night, waking me out of dead sleep. Monica was gone.

Cassie was already talking when I picked up—and not making much sense, even for her. After a few minutes of effort, I finally worked her down to the facts: Something had happened, her house wasn't safe, and I had to meet her someplace ASAP.

"Fisher's Grill in ten minutes," I told her. She was still talking when I hung up.

CHAPTER 15
VERY EARLY

Ten minutes later, I was standing under the green-striped awning outside Fisher's Grill, waiting for Cassie. I could see only a few feet into the parking lot, what with the darkness, heavy rain, and fog, but the only headlights I'd seen so far had gone on by. I was starting to think that I should have offered to go to her house anyway or at least to pick her up. She was a road hazard all by herself when she was upset, and on top of that, the weather was bad.

Finally, though, I heard a familiar screech of tires. Cassie's BMW careened into the lot and slammed into a parking space, almost going right over the concrete bumper. When the car finally stopped moving, I pulled down the brim of my hat, turned up the collar of my raincoat, and went out to meet her. Something was wrong, all right. She was pale and shaky, and she'd had a little trouble getting the car door closed. Moreover, she was standing in a downpour trying to open an umbrella, when it was already too late.

"Run," I told her.

She jumped and looked over her shoulder.

"To get in out of the rain."

"I knew that," she said sharply. But she just stood there.

I took the umbrella, opened it over her head, gave her the handle, and waited.

"You look like a bat in all that black," she snapped.

I let her have that one for free, given the state she was in, and continued to wait.

"I was trying to sleep," she finally said.

"So was I, until you called."

"That's how it started, I mean. I was trying to sleep, and something came in through the window. I couldn't tell what at first. There was all this fog in the room. Then a vampire woman was sitting on my bed."

"A vampire woman?"

"I couldn't see the face. Just the fangs. But she was definitely a she."

I fought very hard not to think what I was thinking. "Sounds like a nightmare. I get those."

"I was awake."

"OK," I said evenly.

"I can prove it. She told me to give you a message. She said to tell you, 'Revelation comes in many shapes.' She said you'd remember. She also said to tell you that she's going to get me too."

Silence. In the light from the restaurant window, I studied Cassie's face. She wasn't making this up, and she didn't have a clue.

"She said she's going to get me too, Devvy."

I smiled, or tried to. "But not on an empty stomach. Shall we?"

⊃⊂

Cassie staked out the most private booth in the restaurant, way back in a corner, and then excused herself for a few minutes. When she finally came back, she looked more like her usual self. I suspected emergency cosmetics.

Then again, a little time on the terra firma of Fisher's might have helped. There was nothing exceptional about the place except its banality. It could have been any 24-hour diner in any city, down to the bored cop drinking coffee at the counter. It was also about as safe a place as there was in the middle of the night. If any undead thing were fool enough to walk through the door, the lighting would burn it to ash.

"Sorry I was gone so long," Cassie said. "They're out of paper towels in there. I had to dry my hair under one of those hand dryers." She slid into the booth, all the way into the corner. "Is that shake for me?"

I pushed the tall glass across the table. "Triple chocolate, with extra chocolate. That OK?"

"Perfect. But you're just having coffee?"

"Well, I ate your other cookie."

She laughed. "Leaving me to starve."

"You could stand to gain a few pounds. I'll order you more cookies, if you want."

"Are you trying to be nice to me?"

"No. I'm trying to get you to shut up for a few minutes." I handed her the spoon. "Have at it. And while you're at it, listen, for once. I've got something to tell you."

಼಼

I told her everything. It took a while, but I told all. Well, all except the sex parts. Cassie listened attentively, without interrupting. I couldn't tell what she was thinking, but she seemed to believe me right from the start. The first time I said Monica's name, in fact, she seemed to understand the rest. What was even stranger, she relaxed visibly. By the time I got to the last part, she was actually smiling.

"So that catches you up, as of last night. She was gone when I woke up—when you called. That's not unusual. She comes and goes as she pleases. But if you believe what I've been telling you, we both know where she was. What we don't know—"

"I believe you," Cassie said abruptly. "I *told* you she was a witch."

"Demon."

"You make a big point of that. Why?"

Good question. Because Monica did, I supposed. "Degrees of evil?"

"If she's *that* evil, she should work for the IRS."

Caught by surprise, I laughed. "It would serve the IRS right. You seem better."

"I *am* better. Things make sense now. This isn't scary now. It's just . . . Monica." Her voice dripped scorn.

"Don't underestimate her, Cass."

"Give her a message from me. Tell *her* not to underestimate *me*." She scraped the last of the syrup out of the bottom of her glass and licked both sides of the spoon. "Are you hungry?"

I checked my watch—a little past four—and then checked out the window. It was still raining and foggy, and generally a good advertisement for staying put for a while. "I could eat. Too early for breakfast, though."

"Forget breakfast; it's still dark. I was thinking along the lines of . . ." She picked up a menu and pondered for a second. "A double chili cheeseburger and fries, with onion rings on the side. And nachos. And a hot-fudge sundae."

I raised both eyebrows.

"With chocolate-chip ice cream," she mused. "Or maybe even—"

"All right, dammit. Me too." I signaled the waitress, who had been watching us with growing suspicion for the past half-hour. "I hope they have Alka-Seltzer in the kitchen."

"You're not shocked?"

"Should I be?"

Cassie smiled. "I should never go to restaurants with anyone else."

"At this hour of the morning," I told her, "you probably never will."

∞

We finally left around six, having left the waitress a major tip for the use of the hall. Just before we got back out in the rain, Cassie stopped me under the awning.

"Thanks for being here, Devvy. You're the best."

"You're welcome, and I am. But don't take this lightly."

"Don't worry. Give me a hug." She seemed to hold on a little longer than usual before letting go. "See you at the coffee machine in a couple of hours."

We got into our cars and passed on the way to the exit. Cassie almost crashed again, for some reason. She waved me over to the side of the parking lot and rolled down her window. I did the same.

"When did you get a Miata?"

"You see it?"

"Yes. But . . ." Cassie's voice trailed off as she thought about it. Then she got it. "Monica."

"Welcome to the funhouse," I told her, and drove off.

∞

Cassie and I had always had one cardinal principle between us: Woe to the third party. We could give each other all the trouble in the world, but God help the fool who tried to give either of us more. I might call her a capitalist breeding sow, but I would carve up anyone who questioned her choice of career or taste in men. Well, her choice of career. She might rake me over coals for the smallest transgression of word, deed, or character, but she would barbecue anyone who tried to do the same.

So I couldn't let Monica get away with whatever she was up to with Cassie.

I lighted into her the second I got home from Fisher's. She

was lounging in bed, watching MTV, wearing my backup black hat and nothing else, and she just laughed. That made me madder, which only made her laugh harder.

Finally, I stalked out of the bedroom and into the bath. There was no point. I couldn't fight this battle on two hours' sleep. Besides, it was time to get ready for work.

I'd just turned on the shower when Monica materialized inches away, causing me to drop the soap.

"You forgot to take your clothes off."

I checked quickly. She was right. So what? "I don't want to catch cold. Get out."

"Pride is a deadly sin. Very attractive on you. Do you like my outfit?"

"Get out of the shower. You're going to ruin my hat."

"I could ruin a lot more than your hat," she said, taking my shirt off.

"You could. But you'd better not. Leave Cassie alone."

"She's a grown woman. She can take care of herself. Take your shoes off."

"I mean it, dammit," I said, trying to oblige.

"I haven't touched her. Literally or otherwise."

"Then don't."

"But I might. You're not jealous, are you?"

That had never occurred to me, and I didn't like the implication one bit. But I didn't want to dwell on it. "Don't waste your time. She doesn't even like you. Besides, she's not even afraid of you. She gave me a message for you, by the way. She said—"

"'Tell her not to underestimate me.' I know. I promise you that I don't." She finished stripping off my soggy clothes and kicked them into a corner of the tub. "I won't hurt her, if that's what you mean. I won't hurt you, either, if you cooperate. Not seriously, anyway. Come here."

"Your word, Monica. No lies this time. Swear it."

She laughed. "What would a demon swear by?"

"Your *word*."

"Very well. If it will please you. I swear by sex, drugs, rock and roll, sex, advertising—"

"You already said 'sex.'"

"—caffeine, and sex that I won't hurt your Cassie."

"She's not *my* Cassie."

She pressed closer, eyes glittering. "We won't talk about it again. Now I advise you to thank me."

"Thank you for what?"

"For my word. For this, too."

What she did next almost made me black out . . . and/or drown, considering the location. I'd seen statistics about the high rate of death in bathtubs and wondered whether this was the cause. It was the death of my defense of Cassie for the time being, anyway. Among other things. Lying in bed an hour later, I took a lighted cigarette from her and smoked it down to the filter.

"You'll hate yourself later," Monica assured me. "But doesn't it feel good?"

I was all the way inside the funhouse now. My guess was that Monica was going to have all the fun.

CHAPTER 16
LATER THAT MORNING

"The trouble with you is that you're weak."

I glared at Cassie for that, but not very hard.

"I don't mean that so much the way it sounds as I do that it's the truth," she continued. "A naked witch gets in running water with you, and you lose your head. How many did you smoke?"

"Just one. Never again, though. It made me sick."

"That was probably from contact with *her*. Did you know that some lizards can poison people just by touch?"

Annoyed, I put down the radio script that she was ostensibly in my office to discuss. "I'm sorry I told you."

"So am I, because now I have to do something about it. You aren't going to kill *me* with secondhand smoke. Wait a minute." She bent over the side of her chair to fish in her attaché. Then she dug something out of a pocket and threw it across the desk. "Here. Put it on."

"Where did you get this?"

"Linda gave it to me. She said you'd relapse sooner or later. Put it on."

"I don't need a patch. I only smoked one."

"She said you'd say that. Just put it on. Don't make me force you."

"Don't make idle threats." I threw the patch back to her. "Here—save this for Linda. *She's* the one who's going to relapse one of these days, you know. It's always the ones who talk the most who—"

"Speaking of talking, shut up," she said, intent on opening the patch pouch. Then she got up, patch in hand, and crossed to my chair.

"What are you doing?"

"Trying to unbutton your shirt so I can stick this on. Let go. Don't make me break a nail."

"*You* let go. This shirt cost $46.50."

"My manicure cost more than that. So I win." She got a good purchase on the third button. I pushed her off it just in time. "Dammit, Devvy, I got no sleep. Don't fight me, or I'll—"

At that moment, the office door opened abruptly, and both of us froze in horror. This had to look really, really bad. Cassie was half in my chair; my shirt was half unbuttoned; and she'd dropped the patch in the struggle, so there was no obvious, ready explanation at hand.

Worse, the person who'd just walked in was Connie the Barbarian.

Cassie let go of my shirt as though it were on fire. I let go of her hands as though they were tarantulas.

"Didn't think anybody was home," the Barbarian said. "Sorry. I knocked."

What with one thing and another, we hadn't heard. This looked bad, all right.

Cassie went back to her own chair, scowling fiercely, while I rebuttoned my shirt. Neither of us said a word.

"Got your invitations to the Halloween party," the Barbarian explained. "Mr. J wanted 'em hand-delivered. Fill out the RSVP part and send it back to Sanchez by Friday."

"On my desk," I said coldly. "Hers, too."

The Barbarian lobbed two invitations over and then leaned back on the mail cart, grinning. She was wearing so much Brut that it stung my eyes from ten feet away.

"Is there something else?"

"You tell *me*, Kerry. How long've you two been going on?"

Outraged, I almost tipped my chair over. "What?"

"C'mon, you can tell. I won't rat on you."

"There's nothing to rat *about*. You didn't see what you think you saw. Cassie was just trying to—"

"Yeah, I bet she was." The Barbarian winked at me—for real this time. "Well, don't sweat it. I can keep a secret."

Then she winked at Cassie, which enraged the woman, who was already cranky enough. She blasted the Barbarian with her heaviest ammunition, calling her everything but a child of God, and then threatened her with several kinds of death, all of them bad. The details all but blew my hair back.

But the Barbarian didn't scare, apparently. She just kept grinning. She was also looking down the front of Cassie's dress.

"Get out," I snarled. "Now."

"Will do. See you at the bars."

"*Out!*"

The Barbarian winked at me again, leered at Cassie one last time, and ambled out.

I followed to make sure that she was gone and to close the door. My hands were shaking, so it took a couple of tries. Cassie, for her part, was the color of chalk.

"It may not be as bad as we think," I lied. "Even if she talks, nobody would believe her. Besides, that's not what really happened."

"Great. *We* know the truth. That'll be a lot of comfort when Kurt finds out."

"He may not find out. But even if he does, he'll believe *our* version, because I'll fire him if he doesn't. People get fired around here for less all the time."

"He *does* like his job," she agreed.

"And if that doesn't work, I can always toss him a model."

"It could work."

"It'll *have* to work," I said grimly. "This can't get out."

We sat in tall silence for a moment. Then Cassie snorted. "Oh, come on—this is crazy. What are we guilty about? Nothing happened. Besides, we've got our reputations to protect us. You're this well-known celibate monster—"

"—and you're not. Not celibate, I mean. You're right. We *do* have our reputations."

"Even though they're lies now."

"Even though they're lies."

Silence.

Finally, I picked up my pen again and reached for the script. "Maybe we should get back to this now."

No response. She was turning something over in her mind. "Cass?"

"If you looked like that," she said, rather absently, "I wouldn't be seen dead with you."

"That would make two of us."

"It's not like I care if you're gay. But at least you don't look gay, or act gay, or—"

"Thanks."

"—smell gay." Seeing my failure to grasp her point, she added, "You don't wear aftershave."

I smiled at her. "One of my many virtues."

"Don't push it, Devvy. I'm already cutting you all the slack I can. You *are* sleeping with that . . . woman. So technically, you're in a gay relationship."

"Technically, hell. She's not a woman."

Cassie looked absolutely disgusted. "Of all the nonsense you've ever told me, and God knows you've told me enough to float a boat, this is the—"

Someone knocked, for a change.

"Wait," I told her, and then called to the door, "In a meeting!"

The door opened anyway, and Jack stuck his head in. "Afternoon, ladies—and I use that word in the very loosest way. Do I hear right, Kerry? Is there news?"

"What news?"

"That's what I need to know. You've been holding out on me, haven't you?"

"What are you talking about?"

"More like *who* I'm talking about. Who you've been doing."

My pen fell out of my suddenly nerveless grip and clattered on the desktop. Meanwhile, Cassie was coughing, for control. "What?"

"Who you're taking to the Halloween party, anyway."

"What?"

"You're usually more articulate than this," Jack remarked. "Disappointing. But I'll overlook it this once, in exchange for information. So who are you taking?"

"I'm not taking anyone. But how would *you* know? I haven't even had a chance to send the RSVP upstairs. In fact, I just got the invitation. It's right . . ." Puzzled, I searched the desk. "It was here a minute ago."

"I just came from upstairs. You must be in parakeet mode again. I saw your RSVP in Sanchez's inbox. It says 'Devlin Kerry and date.'"

Cassie and I exchanged apprehensive glances. We didn't have to wonder; we knew.

"It's all over the fourth floor already. So who is it? C'mon— the party's at the Gold Club this year. Everything goes."

"I haven't sent the form back yet, Jack," I insisted. "Somebody must be playing a practical joke."

"In your handwriting?"

Cassie dropped her own pen.

"Whatever you've got must be catching," Jack commented. "So?"

Clearly, he wasn't going to give up, so I'd have to tell him something—anything—just to make him go away. "If there's anything to find out," I said carefully, "you'll find out at the party."

Jack smiled, showing all his caps. "This is too good not to share. Gotta run." Which he did, almost literally.

"What is she up to?" Cassie asked as the door slammed shut.

"I don't know. So far, only you and I can see her. What would be the point if nobody else can see her?"

"What if she can make them see her?"

I felt a cold skitter of panic. "Maybe she can't."

"I don't know why not. She's a witch."

"Demon."

"Witch. I don't like this. What if we get you a *real* date? That way—"

"There's no 'we' here, Cass. Don't get into any trouble you don't have to get into. This is my problem. I'll handle it."

"You've done a bang-up job up till now," she said dryly.

That stung. "I'm doing the best I can, dammit. It's not like there's any precedent for this situation."

"You have a bigger problem than precedent. You walk into the party with that woman—"

"She's not a woman."

"Stop that," Cassie snapped. "She has all the parts. What do you think people are going to see?"

Good point. I dropped my head onto the desktop and banged it a couple of times.

"Want me to do that for you? A lot harder?"

"You're right, Cass. You're right. I'm dead. This'll do it."

"It'll help." She sighed. "I tried to warn you about being celibate so long. I *told* you something bad would come of it. I don't know whether I can help you now."

"I don't need your help," I growled.

"You need all of my help you can get. I just don't know whether it'll be enough."

"What help can you possibly be? What are you going to do—drive a stake through her heart?"

"Something like that. *If* I decide to do it. I have to think about it first. But I might."

"Don't do me any favors."

"It won't be a favor," Cassie said.

☙❧

Jack came back later that afternoon to tell me he'd sent the whole agency a copy of my RSVP, so that everybody else could enjoy it as much as he had. That was my limit for one day, so I simply walked past him, out of the office, into the elevator, and out to my car.

Monica wasn't home when I got there, and she never appeared that night. Or the next. In fact, I wouldn't see her again for two weeks.

CHAPTER 17
MID-OCTOBER

So St. Devlin, well-known celibate monster, had a date for the Halloween party. That was the word around J/J/G, and the word was the topic du jour for way too many jours. Rather than deny the rumors, I did my best at first to avoid people who would ask about them. That being everyone, though, I finally had to fall back on my old defense.

What date? You know I don't date. No, I don't do that either. Where do you get this stuff? Have you been on the Internet again? On the moon? Under a rock, with all your relatives?

Cassie tried to help the cause by telling people that this date business had to be a Halloween prank, because nothing in the same species would go out with me. She reported that everyone agreed with her, but no one believed her. There was just too much story out there, and it was too much fun to tell. The fact that the party would be at the Gold Club—a so-called show club that owed J/J/G money—was all bonus. What better place for trouble? Kurt had to love this.

True, Kurt had been quiet so far—in the manner of a crocodile, waiting—but I knew that the quiet wouldn't last. Besides, everyone else had more than made up for his lack of collaboration on the stories. Especially Jack. He'd been doing the most creative directing of his life.

What had I been thinking, trying to blow him off with a lame line like "If there's anything to find out, you'll find out at the party"? How had I expected him to take that? The man was a writer . . . sort of. He had imagination, however diseased, and a great big mouth. By the time the story snaked its way back to me a few days later, I was going to the party with a man, a woman, and a Shetland pony—and Heather said she'd heard talk that the pony had a prison record.

"Maybe you'd better stay home," she told me. "It could get ugly if you don't bring the horse."

It could *get* ugly, could it? Really? When? I began to wonder whether Heather had any social antennae at all. I began to wonder whether I shouldn't just get out of town for a while. Fly down to a beach somewhere, maybe. Marinate in Coppertone and margaritas for a couple of weeks, and come back only when it was safe: the day after Halloween.

"You can't go to the beach alone," Cassie said when I told her the plan. "That would look desperate. Besides, I can't go with you. I have too many meetings."

"A vacation? Now?" Jack laughed uproariously. "Forget it, Kerry. No chance. You're going to the party if I have to spend good money to have you arrested and brought there. So what's your costume? What are you going as? A pony trainer?"

Jenner didn't laugh. "You can't take a vacation now, Miss Devlin. Harper said you'd ask. Didn't you just have a vacation a couple of years ago?"

"No Valium," Dr. Shapiro said. "No Xanax. Absolutely no morphine. Have you considered therapy, Devlin?"

That night, I wrote a message on the medicine-cabinet mirror with soap:

YOU WIN. I'M RUINED. NOW COME HOME.

The next morning, I found the answer on the same mirror, written in what might have been blood:

YOU'RE NOT RUINED YET. SEE YOU AT THE PARTY.

Chapter 18
October 30

Danny pulled the rod out and pushed it back in farther down the weight stack. "Attagirl, Dev. Now try it this way."

"No."

"You can do it. It's just one more plate."

"*No*. It's ten more pounds, and this machine's too hard already. Put it back."

"Just give it a shot. Just try one rep. For me."

For him? Pushing wet hair out of my eyes, I gave him an evil look. He had on the Club West pants with a weightlifter's shirt and the very latest neon shoes, which was not how people I did things for dressed. Neither did I care for his dragon tattoo. But at least he didn't wear a baseball cap, the way so many gym rats did, and even though he knew it, he *was* kind of cute.

Besides, Danny was a smart trainer, as trainers went, and he'd done me a lot of good over the years—even in just the past couple of weeks. What with Monica's absence, I'd been hitting the club with a vengeance lately, trying to sublimate and repress and forget. Danny had taken my mood for motivation and had pushed me hard, but no harder than I'd pushed him back. Maybe he knew what he was doing. At those prices, of course, he damned well ought to.

"Let's go. One rep. Want me to start you?"

"I'm not the slacker here," I said in injured dignity and gave the machine a vicious push.

The weight stack wouldn't budge until he helped with the first few inches of lift. Hating him, breathing hard, I put everything into it and slowly, painfully raised the weight.

"Halfway there, Dev. Keep going. Push!"

Two stations down, a very young man in a Chicago Bulls jersey started to pump his machine hard and fast, making the weight stack clang. Startled, I almost dropped my own load.

"No, you don't," Danny said, grabbing the end of one hand grip. "Don't quit on me. Push!"

He might have helped with the weight, which would have been cheating, but I really didn't want to know. At any rate, I pushed that last bit harder and finally made full extension.

"Outstanding. All right, now, down slow."

Slow was out of the question. The weight took itself down and raised me a foot off the bench with it. But I'd done the impossible rep. Damn right outstanding.

"Great work," Danny praised. It was what he always said, after every machine, to every client. "Take a rest. You OK?"

"Yeah. No thanks to *you*."

The Bulls fan, still pumping, let fly with a string of curses. I raised an eyebrow.

Danny shook his head. "Don't pay any attention. He got dumped last night. He's just blowing off."

"Bad form," I remarked.

"Really bad. You never pump. You lift. You lower. Slow."

"I wasn't talking about that kind of form. But that, too." Done toweling off, I took a pull on my water bottle. "OK, what now?"

"Nothing. You're done. Hit the track for six and then go home. Think you can handle that?"

"Don't patronize me, slacker. You think you'll be twenty-five forever, don't you?"

"Actually," he said, "I'm twenty-four."

"Doesn't matter. I have albums older than you. You don't

even know the words to 'Woodstock,' and I'm letting you train me?"

He smiled, unfazed. "Heather McIntyre warned me about you before I took you as a client. She said you talk like this all the time. She said you only do it to people you like, though."

"She told you wrong. How do you know Heather, anyway? I thought she went to Bally's."

"She does. I used to go out with her. No, wait—maybe that was Beth Collins. Or Jeannie something, with the huge—"

"Save us both time. What woman who goes to this club *haven't* you gone out with? Other than me, of course."

"Well, there's Cassie Wolfe. But I'm still working on her."

I laughed, collected towel and water bottle, and got up off the machine. "She'd make roadkill of you, son."

"I'll risk it. That babe is a babe."

" 'Babe,' hell. She's three months older than me."

"Must've been three damn good months." Then he remembered that I paid him. "Hey, listen, I don't mean it like that. It's not like you don't have babe potential. You know? I bet if you'd fix yourself up a little more like—"

"Get out of there while you still can," I advised.

"I didn't mean . . . I mean, you're pretty good-looking and all. I'm not saying you're not. But Cassie . . . well, she's got that . . . those . . . ummm . . . " Guilty, he looked down at his neon shoes. "Oh, hell, forget I said anything. Sorry. Are you mad?"

The very idea that it might worry him almost made me laugh. "No, I'm not mad. But don't do that again. I hate being bored."

"Can't have that," he said, relieved. "You sure you're not mad?"

"I just said I'm not. What is it with you tonight? Is there a full moon or something?"

He brightened visibly. "You know, there *is* a full moon. And tomorrow night's Halloween. How about that?"

How about that indeed. I'd managed to put it out of my mind for an hour, and there it was back. In twenty-four hours or so, I'd be an outcast and maybe out of a job in the bargain. But he didn't have to know that. So I forced on a nasty little smile.

"As a matter of fact, Danny, all day tomorrow is Halloween. I think you ought to make the most of it. You ought to dress up like a personal trainer and scare all the little children. See you next week."

He laughed and pushed me onto the track. Well, OK—I owed him the six laps.

Traffic was heavy for a weeknight. Obeying the signs, I kept to the inside lane, where the walkers were supposed to stay. But the outside lane was so crowded that runners were crossing the white line to pass on the right—dangerous for everyone, not that they cared. Runner scum.

What with having to watch both shoulders, I was a little distracted for the first couple of laps. Then I got caught behind a group of slow walkers, three abreast, with runners boxing me in on both sides. There was nowhere to go, so I slowed down, too, and followed the creepers around the bend.

They were three women, clearly just out of seven-thirty bench class, all of them dolled up in leotards, dangly earrings, and serious makeup. My already-low opinion of aerobics classes dropped another notch. How could it be a workout if you could do it in full makeup?

All right, they looked good, from what I could see in the mirrors around the track. But that was still no excuse for getting on my nerves.

Checking the passing lane again, I saw an unbroken line of runners all the way back around. A couple of very well-groomed men muscled by me on the inside and went on past the femme fatales without a glance.

A thought crossed my mind and then fled. There *were* no gays at Club West.

I passed the finish line to start lap four and resigned myself to finishing the laps at a glacial pace. Couldn't these girlies move any faster than that? They weren't even walking, really; they were sauntering. Sashaying, even. Not only that, but their form was terrible. If they'd just straighten out their strides, they'd have less sway in the hips, which was slowing them by at least—

Oh. They were swaying on purpose, sauntering on purpose, checking the men out, getting checked back. Would I ever catch on to how straight people worked?

Stop that, I warned myself. *You're not necessarily gay. Besides, you haven't even seen Monica for two weeks.*

I tried to think about something else. But it was no use. The three women ahead of me were starting to get really distracting.

The blonde in the middle had caught my eye before, and now I dared to let it linger just a bit. She wore the leotard well, based on what I could see from the back and in the mirrors. Nice legs, too. I'd never really noticed legs before. Of course, I almost never looked at women below the collar, out of fear, guilt, and neurosis, but I had studied the occasional movie star at leisure. I wondered what this woman looked like from the other side.

She was saying something to the shorter woman on her right. What, I couldn't make out, what with the loud music and the thump of sneakered feet all around, but I could almost make out her profile. With a well-manicured hand, she brushed back her long hair, and I caught her scent coming off it. Familiar. I couldn't place it by name, but it was really nice, probably expensive.

Well, I wore good stuff too. But not to work out in, for Christ's sake. What would be the point?

Smiling slightly—women were as much a puzzlement to me sometimes as men had always been—I checked the passing opportunities again as we rounded the next curve. No dice. No matter. I was enjoying the scenery a little bit now, and if that made me a pervert, so what?

Suddenly, up ahead, a runner collided with some geek who was trying to cut across the track to the Universal machines, and a chain reaction began to ripple back. Caught in it, I crashed to the track in a tangle with the blonde and some guy who'd been behind all of us. In the chaos, I saw a hairy hand reach around me to grope the blonde. For a second, I thought about defending her honor.

But in the very next second, she turned around and slapped me. "Pervert!" she shouted.

Stunned, I started to point out that I hadn't touched her—at least, not that way—but it was too late. She was trying to reach around me to grope the boy who'd just groped her.

I made a point of stepping on both of them when I got up off the track. Unfortunately, neither of them noticed.

The phone rang in my sleep. Thinking I was still at work, I answered that way.

"Kerry."

"Wolfe. What terrible phone manners, Devvy."

"Me? You woke me up!"

"Never mind. I have to ask you something."

I reached over to the night table, checked the alarm clock, and scowled. "It had better be important."

"It is. What's in your closet?"

Not amused, I scowled harder. "Is that a trick question?"

"I just got up," she said, "and I found something in my closet that's not supposed to be there. What's in yours?"

"Cass, it's not even morning. I don't care yet."

"I'll come over and look if you don't."

I sighed. "Don't do that. Hold on a minute."

The woman had lost it, most likely. She'd probably found a monster dust bunny or an old boyfriend in her closet and freaked. As for *my* closet, what did it matter? But I would have a look if it would appease her and make her hang up, so I could go back to sleep.

It was hanging on the center hook on the back wall, where I couldn't miss it. Cautiously, I took it down and held it up to the light. Yup, it was what it looked like. I took it back with me to the phone.

"The Halloween fairy was here," I reported. "Shall I assume—"

"She left me an angel costume. What about you?"

"An angel costume? For you? Well, I would never accuse her of typecasting. In fact, up till now, I never thought she had any sense of humor at—"

"Later, dammit. What did she leave you?"

"Well, it's bright red, and it has horns and a pitchfork."

"I hope it fits," Cassie snapped.

"Most likely it would. *If* I were going to wear it. Which I'm not."

"Why? Because it would be redundant?"

She was at full battle stations already, and I hadn't even had coffee yet. "Cut me some slack here. I just got up. Can't we talk about this later?"

"There isn't going to be any 'later' until the party. I've got client calls all day. It's now or never."

"What is?"

"What we're going to do about the witch. I just talked to her."

That woke me right up. "What?"

"You have to take her to the party tonight, Devvy."

"I can't take her. Are you crazy? And what do you mean, you just talked—"

"Remember I said I'd have to think about helping you out of this mess? I've thought, and I'm going to help. You're going to owe me *huge*. But first, you have to take her to the party."

"I can't. It would look like a date."

"Exactly."

Maybe something was wrong with the phone. I held the receiver away and shook it a couple of times. Faintly, I heard Cassie still talking. "Still here. Say that again?"

"You heard me. You have to play along just this once. Trust me. Besides, nothing very bad's going to happen."

"Spoken like Custer. 'What Indians?'"

"You want to get rid of her, don't you?"

Long, long silence on my end.

"Devvy? Don't think. Just answer. Do you want to get rid of her?"

"Yes," I said, uncertainly.

"Thank God. I was afraid for a minute there that you'd lost what was left of your mind. See you tonight."

"Wait a minute. I don't even know if she'll be around. I haven't seen her for—"

"She'll be there. In fact, she'll meet you there. See you tonight."

"But—"

"And wear the costume," Cassie said, making it an order. Then she hung up.

I hung up, too, and tossed the costume on the bed. No sense even trying to get back to sleep now. Might as well make coffee, take a shower, and get ready for work.

Two steps into the bathroom, I stopped. The medicine-cabinet mirror was broken.

⊂⊰⊱⊃

An hour later, still shaken, I opened the garage door and got another bad surprise: The Miata was gone. Parked in its place was my old MG, with the new top that I'd sent it to the shop for three months ago.

"Monica!" I shouted.

No answer, not that I'd expected one. Damn. I'd really loved that car.

Swearing from the heart, I got in and started the MG to let it run. It needed a couple of minutes in the morning. While the car warmed up, I checked my tape collection—intact, except for the Go-Go's tape that had perished the night of the wreck—

and pushed *American Fool* into the deck. Then I adjusted the mirrors.

For a second, I thought I saw a pair of glittering red eyes in the side mirror. But it was only a glimpse, and it could have been my imagination, after all. Between Monica and Cassie, my nerves were shot.

I cranked up the tape and got out of there as fast as the MG would go.

◕◔

The rest of the day could have been worse. Jenner, who loved Halloween, was off supervising the decoration of the party site. Lemminglike, Jack and most of the rest of management went with him. That meant no meetings to speak of, which in turn meant that people could actually get work done. For my part, I dug in behind a closed, locked door and drained the swamp without seeing a single alligator all day.

Cassie, after all, was out of the office. Jack was off drinking and watching people string crepe paper. Even Kurt was no problem. He was at his desk, happily sorting through 8x10 glossies of girl models. I'd promised that he could run the auditions for his Hairport spot, in exchange for staying away from me all day.

But day was one thing. All bets were going to be off when the sun went down.

CHAPTER 19
HALLOWEEN NIGHT

At eight-thirty sharp—only half an hour late—I parked the MG on the street, buttoned my black greatcoat to the chin, and walked toward the Gold Club as slowly as possible without actually going in reverse. There'd been no sign of Monica all day, not since that weirdness in the morning, but I knew that she was close by, waiting. It was zero hour. I wondered whether whatever was going to happen tonight would hurt.

Never mind. The less thinking now, the better.

Plastic pitchfork in one hand, I pushed open the lobby door with the other and nodded to the Grim Reaper stationed at the coat check. Some computer wonk from Operations, I figured. He was wearing an Ironman Timex. Encouraged by the notice, he reached out to take my coat.

Defensively, I drew it tighter. I had every intention of wearing it all night. As Cassie had hoped, the devil costume fit, but it was a tight fit.

He motioned again—and for emphasis, chopped a couple of times with his sickle.

"Troll," I growled, showing him the business end of my pitchfork. Then I went on past him through the revolving door that led to the club proper.

Halfway around, Monica materialized next to me. When we came out the other side, she was wrapped around me like a cobra. Fortunately, the place was dark except for some red mood lighting. Maybe no one would notice.

"Let go!" I whispered fiercely.

"A fine hello after two weeks," she said. "I thought you'd be happier to see me. I'm certainly happy to see *you*. Lovely party, isn't it?"

Squinting in the crimson dark, I tried to see whether it was. Slowly, the scene came into focus. We were standing on a stair landing over the main floor of the club, looking into the maw of an awful bacchanalia straight out of *The Masque of the Red Death*, minus only the death—I hoped. Even scarier was the way that Jenner had caused the place to be done over for tonight, complete with smoke machines, candelabra, and howling Gothic organ. I wondered whether this was what churches were like in Hell. Back where the altar might have been was a colossal mirrored bar, which I guessed would run out early, by the look of the crowd. Even in the dark and the smoke, I could see a few revelers already down for the count. People were stepping around them, but some of those people were weaving.

You had to give Jenner credit—the man belonged in a cage, but he knew how to throw a certain kind of party. The staff was still talking about the Fourth of July party at the lake two years ago. You don't see strippers on water skis every day. Neither do you let the fireworks crew have a whole keg of beer, if you're smart, because you can bet that they'll burn down a boathouse, which they did. Which may have been why J/J/G didn't celebrate the Fourth anymore.

"Hey, Kerry! That you?"

With some trouble, I located the source of the voice: a giant rat, lumbering up the stairs with a drink in each hand. I thought it might be an art director.

"Kerry! You were supposed to bring a date. I had fifty bucks on—" Suddenly, he dropped both drinks. "Jesus God! Is *she* with *you*?"

His voice was very loud, and as evil luck would have it, at that moment the music wasn't. Every head in the place snapped in our direction. It was too late to run; we'd been seen. More accurately, Monica had been seen.

I gave her a good hard look myself . . . and my jaw dropped. I'd seen her before, of course, but there was something different about her tonight. Her dress seemed to be tighter, if that were possible. It also seemed to be . . . well, wet. The fabric stuck to her like paint, and even as dark as the room was, I could see . . .

Well, everything.

She smiled at my expression, with a flash of fangs, and then took my arm. "They've heard rumors. Let's see whether everything they've heard is true."

If I had ever hoped to live down the Rumours ad, all hope died as Monica pulled me down the stairs, past the dumbstruck rat, and into the crowd, which parted like the sea. Every eye in the house followed us. Even in the dim light, I could pretty well tell from the faces what people had heard—and what they thought of the truth. One woman in a mermaid costume drew her tail up sharply as we passed by. I suddenly wondered whether I'd ever be welcome in a women's restroom again.

Then I saw Kurt.

Monica pressed even closer. "Isn't that sweet? He's drooling on his pearls."

"Sweet" wasn't quite the word for it. Kurt was in full drag, a terrible vision in pink taffeta with a flower garland on his head and drool on his chin. He looked like a demented bridesmaid, really, which didn't surprise me but did worry me some. I would have to worry about him later, though. A few feet away, some dimwit started wolf-whistling, with feeling.

"God damn," a male voice complained. "How did Kerry ever get lucky?"

Another male voice, even closer, shot back, "Does Kerry even know *how* to get lucky?"

Raucous laughter. That did it. I pulled Monica to a stop and raised my voice to address the party as a whole.

"I'm only going to say this one time. Yes, she's my date. She's with me. I'm with her. We're together. My date is a woman, and I have personally seen the evidence. Now all of you mind your own business. Kurt, wipe your chin."

The room erupted in joyous horror. Out of the corner of my eye, I saw Kurt's wife, in a man's three-piece suit, wiping his chin with her tie.

"Outed at Halloween," I muttered to Monica. "You're good."

"Actually, my little devil, I'm sensational. Shall we?"

We started walking again. I took the lead this time, making straight for the bar. Monica smiled brightly to left and right, enjoying the naked attention. I did not smile. In fact, I was trying to look as dangerous as possible. When we reached the bar, I simply pointed the pitchfork at a couple in his-and-hers nun costumes, and they ran for their lives.

"Whatever's fastest," I told the bartender.

He didn't appear to have heard a word. He was too busy goggling at Monica.

Was this Club West all over again? I leaned all the way into his face. "Two of something. *Now.*"

"Nonsense," Monica told him. "Champagne. The best you have."

I started to override the order, but she wet her lips at him . . . and the bartender dived into the little refrigerator and came up with an expensive black bottle. In his rush to open it, he shot himself in the forehead with the cork and fell like a cut pine.

"Moron," I said, not bothering to lower my voice.

"But a moron who shares your taste," Monica replied, not

bothering to lower hers, either. Wary, I looked around to see whether anyone was close enough to be listening.

Cassie was. She was standing alone a few feet away, done up to perfection in the angel costume, a gold halo floating over her golden hair; the wings looked real. In fact, she was absolutely gorgeous. She was looking directly at me with no expression on her face at all.

She held my eyes for an instant and then walked off without a word.

Monica laughed and traced the sharp edge of a fingernail down my jugular. It hurt.

⋯

Around eleven, Chip and his date hit the bar, where I'd dug in for the rest of the evening. "How're you doing?" he asked.

"I've had better Halloweens. Hi, Deanna."

"Hi yourself. Nice costume, I think. Are you ever going to take your coat off?"

"No."

"Suit yourself," Chip said. "Seems pretty warm in here to me, though." He motioned to the vacant barstools. "May we?"

"Free country."

They sat and ordered more drinks. Then Troy and Heather happened along and decided to do the same.

"So, Dev, where's your date?" Troy asked.

"In a cave somewhere, I suppose. Sharpening her fangs."

"Those are great fangs," Deanna agreed. "They really look real. Where did she get them?"

I shrugged. There wasn't time.

"You two are quite the power couple tonight," Troy continued. "I hear everybody's been wanting words with you."

"Everybody's *had* words with me. I had to give up this

drinking-and-mingling business an hour ago, in self-defense." Moodily, I swirled the ice in my Evian-with-a-twist. "I've heard from damn near every county—and every single nimrod in Human Resources. It's been quite an education."

"Oh, come on," Chip said. "It can't be *that* bad. We're an ad agency. We're all pretty PC, if you want to—"

"It's all *been* PC. Well, mostly, if you don't count the born-again crowd."

Troy frowned. "We have born-agains? Where?"

"Just swing a dead cat."

Deanna looked horrified.

"Just an expression," I told her. "You know. 'You can't swing a dead cat without hitting—'"

"I like cats," she protested.

"Sorry. Bad choice of words." What did Chip see in this one? I turned back to Troy. "Anyway, I've heard all about fire and brimstone, and the Garden of Eden, and Armageddon, and the wages of sin. That attitude, I can almost understand. Those halfwits believe it. They've heard it all their lives. How can they not? But as for the *rest* of these people . . . the Correctness Police—"

"Uh-oh," Heather said.

"—it would be better if they'd just be honest. They think the same thing; they just won't say so."

"You're sure you're not projecting?" Troy asked, concerned.

I ignored that. "Nobody says they think it's wrong or immoral or *weird,* or even that it makes them uncomfortable. They just tell me how *difficult* my life will be from now on and how *other* people won't understand. The worst part is that Monica was standing right next to me every time, and they *still* said it. She just smiled."

"It's just a few people," Troy said. "Relax. It's not that bad."

                                       K. Simpson

"Compared with what?" I drained the glass and motioned to the bartender—now heavily bandaged—for another.

"Well, *we* haven't been on you about her," he said.

"Or us," Chip added.

"No," I admitted. "Not you. Just the Baptists, the hypocrites, and the Dick-and-Jane crowd. Mostly the Dicks."

Heather, who'd been scanning the room behind us, cut off the laughter by clearing her throat. "Speaking of . . ."

We all turned, following her glance. Kurt was approaching, with Peg. Deanna giggled.

"Ah. The Great Satan." Kurt clapped a hand on my shoulder. "How's my favorite deviant?"

I regarded his hand with distaste. "Big talk from a man wearing purple nail polish."

"It's not purple," he said grandly. "It's plum."

"Doesn't go with the dress, boyfriend," Troy advised.

"That's what I tried to tell him," Peg said. "I said, 'Honey, you can't wear pink after Labor Day, and you can't wear plum with pink anyway, so why don't you just wear the cowboy costume like we talked about?'" She turned to Heather, expectant of girl talk. "I was going to be Dolly Parton."

Heather regarded the front of her own costume mournfully. "So was I." Laughter.

"Prisoners of sex roles," Kurt remarked. "But *you* don't have that problem, do you, boss?"

Not wanting to touch him, I pushed his hand off my shoulder with the pitchfork.

"People have been at her all night," Chip explained. "The Holy Roller crowd, anyway."

Kurt feigned surprise. "Really? The troglodytes. You'd think they'd never seen Dev with a vixen-bitch sex goddess before. Speaking of sex, boss, how is she? In the rack, I mean. Or even in the—" Peg snapped his bra straps—hard, by the sound. "Ow!"

"Somebody ought to tell her," Deanna said, glaring at Kurt. "I'd want to know if somebody was talking about *me* like that. Want me to tell her, Dev?"

"I don't know where she is. She didn't say where she was going."

"Oh, I just saw her a few minutes ago. She was talking to Cassie Wolfe."

I instantly set my glass down on the bar so hard that everyone else's glasses rattled and spun around on my barstool. But before I could get completely vertical, Monica showed up. She abruptly put me back down and then sat on my lap.

Everyone pretended not to notice—everyone except Kurt, who was maneuvering to get a better look down Monica's gown. Peg snapped his bra straps again.

"I missed you terribly," Monica said. "Did you miss me? Did you miss *this*?"

I jumped; she'd just bitten my ear. "I wish you wouldn't do that."

"But darling, you usually love it."

The group tried not to laugh, not very successfully. "She's just doing that to give you bad ideas," I told them.

"Too late," Chip said. This time, they all laughed out loud.

"You people must not understand the situation," I said grimly. "My date is a woman. And I've done a lot more with this woman than just date her."

"I'll say," Monica murmured in my ear—and then bit it again. I fended her off as far as possible and checked the faces around us. All smiles.

I didn't get it. "Aren't you supposed to be outraged? This is Wal-Mart Nation. Don't they still stone deviants around here?"

"Well, I guess we're just an outpost of perversity," Heather said.

Kurt grinned. "Don't say that in front of her; she'll use it in an ad. I'll bet she could even get bestiality out of it. How about this? 'Pet Depot: Your friendly neighborhood outpost of perversity.'"

"'Where your pet can *really* be an animal,'" Heather added.

"Pets can be gay?" Deanna asked.

"I hear," Monica whispered, "that some baby ducks are."

I almost had a coronary on the spot.

"You're as red as your costume, Dev," Chip observed. "Come on—lighten up. We're just playing."

"What are we playing?" Cassie asked, right at my shoulder.

I jumped again. Where had she come from? More to the point, why was she asking Monica that question?

There was no way that anything good could come of this. But before I found out for sure, there was a terrible commotion at the top of the stairs, drawing everyone's attention away. Management had landed, fresh from a private party somewhere, and they'd brought along a few of their little friends. Most of the suits were actually *in* suits, but not Jenner. Definitely not Jenner. He was a giant green glow-in-the-dark condom—and a drunk one, at that.

"I heard he was going to dress up like the Washington Monument," Cassie said dryly, "but then someone told him that the innuendo might offend the ladies."

I smiled at her, appreciating the wisecrack. But she didn't smile back. She was staring at me now, with that same emotionless expression.

"Is this thing on?" Jenner asked, tapping a microphone. "Am I on?"

One of the agency's accountants steadied him. "You're on, Mr. Jenner. You're hooked into the house PA."

"I'm on? Everybody can hear me?"

"Loud and clear, sir," the accountant said.

Jenner held the mike to his mouth with both hands and all

but shouted into it, just to make sure. "If you can hear me out there, I want to thank you all for coming tonight. So to speak." Guffaws around the room except in my group, and especially on the landing.

Jenner grinned, encouraged. "Hope you all found the bar all right. I know *I* did. Can everybody see me all right?"

More laughter.

"I thought I'd practice safe party."

Laughter again, but a little on the strained side now.

"I'm coming down now," he said, "and I'm going to dance with the prettiest girl in the place, whoever she is."

One of the party on the stair landing whispered to him. "The prettiest girl in the place except for my bride," Jenner amended. Then he lurched down the stairs, hotly pursued by suits.

"Where *is* No. 5?" Heather asked. "Do you see her up there?"

"I think she's the hooker," Chip said.

"Which hooker?"

While they tried to sort out the candidates, Kurt scuttled over to the foot of the stairs and called up to Jenner. "Sir? You want to dance with the prettiest girl?"

"Who's that woman?" Jenner asked. "Jesus. Or is that a he? If that's a she, why doesn't she shave?"

"I'm a he, sir. I'll give you my card later. But first, I want you to know that the prettiest girl in the room is sitting at the bar right this minute. She's in a long black dress, and I promise that you can't miss her."

I would already have been across the room fixing Kurt's little pink wagon had Monica not been sitting on my lap . . . and had Chip and Troy not immediately stepped in to block the way.

"That evil mothering sonuvabitch," I snarled. "I'll tear his heart out. I'll rip out his spleen. I'll—"

"Later, precious," Monica said, adjusting my costume horns.

"Precious?" Deanna asked Chip.

Then Jenner found the bar, and us, and rocked back on his heels in shock. "My God, Daniels! Do you see that?"

"Yes, sir," the accountant said unhappily. "She's sitting on Miss Kerry's—"

"What maracas!"

Outraged, I tried to rise to defend Monica's honor—*somebody* had to—but she reached back and wrapped her arms around me, effectively getting me in a bodylock. Meanwhile, everyone on my side except Cassie cleared out, the cowards.

"I want to know this young lady. As soon as possible. Hold this, somebody." Jenner held his drink out behind him, knowing that someone would take it. Someone did. Then he advanced on Monica. "I don't believe we've met. I'm Nathaniel Winslow Jenner III. Do you work for me?"

The suits eyed him nervously. I took firm hold of Monica, just to be safe, but whether I was trying to protect her or Jenner was a toss-up.

"I hope you'll favor me with a dance," Jenner said, already reaching for her. "I hope you *can* dance in that dress. You look—wait a minute. You're not moving. Who's got you? Who's this?"

"Who is whom?" Monica asked sweetly.

"Whoever's under you. Whomever. Whoever." He swatted at my restraining arm. "Let go, you horse's ass. It's only for one dance, probably."

I didn't budge. Jenner, in no mood to be thwarted, tried to pull my arm out of its socket. But before he could do any medical-grade damage, Jack pushed through the crowd that was gathering around the bar.

"Sorry I'm late," he said. "Client threw up all over the Jag, and I had to call—Jesus! Who's the babe?"

Jack couldn't see me from that angle, but unfortunately, I could see him. Batman was not a look that worked on a man who didn't work out.

"Mind your own business, Harper," Jenner warned him. "I saw her first." He pulled on my arm again. This time, it hurt. Monica just laughed and slapped his hand away.

"You don't want to dance?" Jenner asked, not following. "Are you with somebody? Is that it?"

I felt Cassie's stare and looked over. Slowly, she nodded.

You've got to play along, she'd said. All right, dammit. This had gone far enough. I'd play.

"She's with me, Mr. Jenner," I said.

"Who said that?" he asked, suspicious. "That sounds like a girl."

"It is a girl." With that, I leaned around Monica into Jenner's—and Jack's—line of vision. "Devlin Kerry. Your associate creative director in charge of sex."

Jack practically swallowed his cigar. Jenner, not sober enough to process in real time, just stared—first at me, then at Monica, then at me again.

"No," he finally said. "This is a Halloween joke. Trick or treat. Am I right?"

Monica smiled at him mockingly and got down off my lap. Then she pulled me to my feet and kissed me—for a lot longer than was necessary to answer the question, really.

I was dimly aware of whoops, catcalls, and a few boos. Over that noise, also dimly, I could hear Jack swearing a blue streak. But Monica was putting all kinds of English and her whole body into the kiss, so I was a little preoccupied at the moment.

Finally, Jenner yanked the tail of my coat, just hard enough to break my concentration a little. "That's going too far. It's not funny. You're trying to make me look like a jackass. I won't be made a jackass. What the hell's your name again? Derry?

Kevlin?" He stamped his foot. "Stop that right now. Right now. I'm your boss. Derry!"

Reluctantly, I disengaged. "We'll finish this later," I told Monica.

"You're not afraid?" she asked.

"Nothing else can happen now. Absolutely nothing. So there's nothing to be afraid of."

Monica smiled—genuinely, for the first time since I'd known her. It made her look almost human. To my shock, in that moment, I felt something almost like love for her . . . and saw it reflected in her eyes.

Which, astonishingly, were no longer red, but a very vivid blue.

"Derry!" Jenner shouted.

Lost in contemplation of Monica, who was still smiling, with that look still in her eyes, I paid no attention.

Jenner yanked on my coattail again. "Derry!"

Reluctantly, I turned back to Jenner. "Sir? You brayed?"

"She can't say that to you, sir," Jack told him helpfully.

"That's right, Derry. You can't say that to me."

"I just did," I pointed out.

Jenner turned purple. Jack tapped him on the shoulder again. "You can fire her, sir."

"That's right. I can fire her. Derry?"

"Sir?"

"You're fired!"

"You can't fire me," I said calmly.

"I can't? Why in hell can't I?"

"I refuse to be fired by a fluorescent prick."

It took a second for it to sink in. Then people started to howl in appreciation, and as word spread through the room, the crowd around the bar began to grow. Jack glared at me. Jenner blinked, disbelieving, and then grabbed one of the agency's lawyers by the collar.

"Hotchkiss? What did she say? Why can't I fire her?"

The lawyer cleared his throat, perhaps to buy time. "She said she'll sue you for wrongful dismissal."

"Can I afford it?"

"Not until next quarter," he said.

"Well, what *can* I do? I have to do something. She just kissed a girl. In front of everybody. I'll bet she's slept with her, too. Jesus, I can't have that in my agency. It's bad for business. Let me fire her. To hell with the money. We'll just raise rates on the clients again. Besides, I *want* to fire her. It's my—"

"Then you'll have to fire me, too, Mr. Jenner," Cassie said.

I spun around. She was standing at my shoulder again, perfectly calm.

"Stay out of this, Cass," I told her.

She ignored me, fixing a steady gaze on Jenner, who looked stumped.

"Why would I want to fire *you*, Miss Wolfe?" he asked. "You're the best-looking girl on my payroll."

"Now, just a damn minute," a female voice protested, and the crowd began to laugh.

"Admirable, Miss Wolfe," Monica said. "Now finish it."

I spun in the other direction. Now Monica was on the front line with us. "You stay out of this too," I warned.

"No, Devvy," Cassie said. "This is between her and me now."

"*I'm* between the two of you, and I'm not letting you do anything crazy. I think you're both—"

"Don't think," Monica told me. "It only confuses you. Just let her do what she has to do. We came to a final agreement about that a little while ago."

"What? What agreement?"

"Somebody tell me what all the whispering's about!" Jenner demanded.

"Get out of the way, Devvy," Cassie said.

"Not on your life. Don't make deals with her, Cass. You know what she is. It isn't—"

They both rounded on me, looking equally menacing. Involuntarily, I took a long step back.

"Go on," Monica told Cassie.

She regarded Monica coolly and then turned back to Jenner. "You can't fire Devvy because she slept with a woman." Then, sotto voce, but sharply, to Monica: "And I mean *slept*. Past tense."

Monica laughed. I could see the blue lights dancing in her eyes even from a distance.

"I don't have to fire her, Miss Wolfe," Jenner was saying. "Hotchkiss here says I can just take away her parking space and send her to counseling, and that'll be—"

"You can't fire Devvy because she slept with a woman," Cassie repeated, "because if you fire her for that, you'll have to fire me, too."

Instant, total silence, as deafening as a bomb. My knees gave way. Chip and Deanna barely made the catch in time. Then Kurt shattered the silence, horribly: "Yeeeehaw!"

Yeeeehaw? Insolent little hilljack sonuvabitch. I promised myself to have his heart and spleen the second I could walk again.

Cassie and Monica paid no attention, standing calmly where they were, waiting for Jenner to hear what Cassie had just said. Finally, he did, sort of.

"But that's impossible!" he shouted. "You're beautiful! You have long hair! You have—"

"If you believe everything you see, Mr. Jenner," Cassie said, "you *are* a fluorescent prick."

The audience liked it the second time, too. Jenner, however, did not. He went into an angry huddle with the suits. Meanwhile, Jack was shoving through the crowd to Cassie, determined to get to the bottom of this, by God.

"I can't have heard you right, Wolfe. You *can't* have slept with a girl. Hell, you haven't even slept with *me* yet. Kerry put you up to this, didn't she?"

"She doesn't have that much imagination," Cassie replied.

I would have argued the point had Chip not showed me his fist by way of warning. Maybe everyone was right tonight. Maybe it *was* best to stay out of things.

"I still don't believe you," Jack was telling Cassie. "It doesn't make sense. *You* slept with a girl? *You*?"

"Believe me."

"You got naked with a girl?"

"As a jaybird." She leaned closer to him, confidentially. "You know what else, Jack? It was great."

Two or three beats of very pregnant silence. Then Jack slammed his cigar to the floor in a passion and yanked Jenner out of the huddle.

"I'm in a meeting, Harper!"

"You're adjourned, you bastard!" Jack shouted—and punched him in the nose.

Jenner went down in a green heap. For a couple of heartbeats, everyone froze.

And then all hell broke loose all over the club, in an absolute orgy of violence. Thanks to Jack's example, and perhaps even more to all that alcohol, people were busy getting actual pieces of people they'd hated for years—which, in an ad agency, added up to a lot of hate.

"This is *your* fault!" Jack was howling, windmill-punching Jenner while a few of the suits tried—not very hard—to pull him off. "You son of a bitch! It's your fault!"

"What do you suppose *that's* about?" Chip asked.

I wrenched away from him and Deanna. Jenner was fighting back now, and Wife No. 5 was screaming and flailing at Jack with her little evening purse. In the odd clarity that sometimes comes during chaos, I noticed that she really *was* dressed like a hooker and that the costume fit her too well to be a costume. I also noticed that the Hardware City girl was right behind her, about to whack her in the head with the spike of a shoe. At any other time, I would have found the situation irresistible.

But this was no time for spectator sport. Monica was smiling rather mockingly at Cassie, who still had no expression on her face, and getting back between them to thwart someone—anyone—seemed like a good idea.

"You can handle it from here, can't you?" Monica asked Cassie as I approached.

"I can handle *her*. I never want to see you again."

"Maybe you won't." Monica turned to kiss my cheek. "Love," she said.

The next instant, she was gone. No flash of fire, no puff of smoke—just gone. Tentatively, I poked the pitchfork into the empty space. Nothing.

Fortunately, I was the only person who'd noticed. No one had been paying the slightest attention, of course, with all those brawls going on . . . no one, that is, except Cassie.

"Never mind that. We need to talk," she was saying. "In private, right now. Come with me."

"I wish I'd wake up now," I said, more to myself than to her.

"You're awake. This way."

Cassie pulled me past the bar, pushing fighters and spectators out of the way as we went, making for a private room in the back. Inside, a pudgy spider was sleeping it off. Cassie jerked him to his feet.

"There's a fight outside," she informed him. "Jenner and Jack Harper. I think there's blood on the floor. Hurry and see before somebody dies."

The spider hurried. Cassie slammed the door behind him.

"Trick or treat?" I asked, experimentally.

"This is all your fault, you know." She adjusted her wings, which had gotten a little lopsided in the crush. "I blame her more than I do you, but you're here and she's not—thank God!—so I'm going to blame you."

"Level with me, Cass. That was a trick?"

"It was no trick. I slept with a woman."

I eyed her narrowly. She didn't even blink. "My God. You're serious, aren't you?"

"It was in college," she said. "It was just one time. It just sort of *happened*. Do you remember screw-top wine?"

"Strawberry Hill?"

"That's the one."

I winced, remembering it only too well. "Well, that would explain it. You were legally insane."

"That's what I told myself for a long time. Then I came to work at J/J/G. That was six years ago. Remember? My first morning, I went to the break room and saw this lunatic banging on the coffeemaker with a stapler, trying to make it *brew* faster. Then you looked up—"

"No," I said, disbelieving.

"—and I thought, 'If she's funny, I'm in trouble.' Do you remember what you said? You said you were sorry to be so crude, but your doctor wouldn't let you take coffee intravenously anymore. So *I* said—"

"*You* said your doctor told you the same thing about men," I told her, slowly, "and I thought, 'I'm in trouble.'"

Cassie looked stunned.

"I swear to God, Cass, I'd forgotten all about that until this very second."

"You *repressed* it, you mean. All these years. All six years I've known you. *Damn* you."

Silence. Then I understood all the rest, and smiled.

"Your halo's crooked," I told her.

"Well, so is yours."

Still smiling, I adjusted her costume halo.

"I hate you," she said softly.

"I hate you too. What do you want to do about it?"

We were a fraction of an inch from what she wanted to do about it when we heard a suspicious noise. "Quiet!" she whispered. "Where's your pitchfork?"

Not following her logic, but not thinking all that straight at the moment anyway, I handed it over. She got a good grip on it, tiptoed to the door, carefully took hold of the doorknob—and then twisted and pulled sharply. Kurt, Heather, Chip, and Troy tumbled into the room, landing at her feet.

"You!" she shouted, menacing them with the pitch-fork. "How long have you been there? How much did you hear?"

Chip, Troy, and Heather lost no time scrambling up off the floor. Kurt was still floundering around in all those ruffles. Pointedly, I let him pick himself up.

"There's already been a lot of talk about firing people tonight," Cassie told Chip. "You're on thin ice, mister. What did you hear?"

"Well . . ."

"Well, what?"

"Nothing."

"The truth."

"Practically nothing. But don't look at me. It was Kurt's idea."

I took one step toward Kurt, who tried to escape and promptly broke a heel, going back down in a pink taffeta heap. By the thunk he made, I figured he'd be down for a while.

"What do you want me to do with him? Give him a sex change?" I asked Cassie hopefully.

"I wouldn't want to watch that. Besides, it wouldn't be bad enough. Why don't we give him to Connie the Barbarian while he's all dolled up?"

"She's here," Heather volunteered. "In a Teletubbies costume."

"With a date?" I asked.

"Well, she's with another Teletubbie. They were making out on the dance floor."

"Really? And did the Baptists call the National Guard? Did the Teletubbies get any of this grief about deviance that's been going around tonight?"

"Well, Dev," Heather said, "at least Connie didn't lie about what she is."

Cassie had to practically tackle me to keep me from hurting her.

Kurt sat up in the corner, rubbing his head. "Interesting. She's extra-touchy tonight. I wonder what *that* means."

"Maybe it means," Troy said thoughtfully, "that nothing's happened yet."

The others looked at him, eyes bright.

"You think . . . ?" Heather asked.

"Let go, Cass," I demanded. "I can probably kill them all."

Cassie held on tighter. She was practically on my back.

"Give me a hand up," Kurt told Troy, who did. "Thanks. Now, where are we? We seem to have a situation here. Let me ask Dev a question and see if we can get to the bottom of it. Got a good hold on her, Cassie?"

"That depends on your question."

Kurt laughed. "It's a simple question. Won't take a second to answer. Who's your date tonight, boss?"

There was no way to tell the truth, and there was no time to tell a convincing lie. So I decided—as I so often did—to split the difference.

"Monica? Christ, you idiot, she's not really my date. She's a Halloween trick."

Kurt clearly hadn't been expecting that answer. "A trick?"

"I figured it would be just your speed," I said, warming to the tale. "It was worth the money just to see the look on your face. Maybe next year, I'll hire Bouncing Betsy. Or whatever Jenner's married to next year. I might even—"

Cassie cut me off with a jab in the ribs. "Don't listen to her. She's crazy."

"We know that," Troy said. "The question is whether we believe her. Heather? What do you think?"

"It could be true," she mused. "That woman *was* awfully over the top."

"I couldn't agree more," Cassie muttered.

Kurt laughed. "Pity. I would've loved to imagine the two of them together. She looks just like what you'd have to figure Dev's sexual fantasies are like. Of course, I suppose that there are other fantasies. Do you like blondes, boss? Would you like us to leave?"

"In a box, if I get my way. Get out."

"Any special reason?" he asked.

I was about to give him any number of special reasons when Cassie let go and stepped between us. "Give it up, Devvy. They're not *that* stupid. It's too late." Then she turned to Kurt. "Get out before I kick you out. She was just about to kiss me."

A split-second of silence. Then Kurt rebel-yelled again and threw open the door. The costumed bodies of at least a dozen eavesdroppers fell into the room. Cassie and I leaped back in shock.

Kurt, glorying in a moment that he'd obviously been waiting for, laughed at us and then called through the open door to the party outside, "Ladies and gentlemen, I have your winner: Dev and Cassie!"

Groans and cheers went up in the room, and just outside it, and money began changing hands.

"They were betting on this?" Cassie asked me, indignant.

"Settle up at the bar!" Kurt shouted. The room emptied as fast as it filled. Considerately, Chip backtracked to shut the door—and ducked just in time to miss the pitchfork, which Cassie sailed over his head.

"They were betting on this?" she repeated.

"Of course they were betting on this. They're a goddamn pack of swine. They're probably out there making book right now on what time I'll kiss you."

"Want to bet?"

I checked my watch. "It's almost midnight. What time do you want?"

"Right now," Cassie said, and kissed me.

The Fourth of July when the boathouse burned down, I'd been standing close enough to get soot on my clothes. But the heat of that fire was nothing compared with this one—and the damnedest thing was, neither was Monica. If this was how it was going to start with Cassie, I was definitely going to end up dead.

What the hell.

Finally, Cassie backed off a tiny bit. "I think this is the part where somebody says, 'Your place or mine?'," she murmured.

"My place is closer."

"Good. Your place. What time is it?"

What did it matter? I checked again. "Midnight. Why?"

"Monica owes me $100. She bet me you wouldn't kiss me until after midnight."

"That doesn't count," I told her. "*You* kissed *me*."

"You kissed me back."

"You started it."

"It counts as a kiss."

"Does this mean we're still going to fight?"

"Until we die," Cassie promised, and closed back in. "I'm going to make your life a living hell, Devlin Kerry."

"Can't wait," I said.

CHAPTER 20
NOVEMBER 1

Cassie wanted to watch the sun come up from out on the deck, so I went along with her. There wasn't much to see yet except white: fog rolling off the lake, mist drifting over the frosted lawns, steam rising from our coffee mugs. It wasn't any too warm yet, either. All I had on was the black robe, and I was freezing.

But then I looked at her, wearing only my black greatcoat, apparently impervious to the temperature. She was standing at the rail like a Viking queen surveying her lands, hair blowing lightly in the icy wind, and suddenly I didn't feel the cold anymore.

"You would make a fantastic photograph," I told her. "Always, but especially right now."

She laughed, caught by surprise. "Sweet talk from you? This *is* a cold day in Hell."

"Cold enough." I set my mug on the rail and kissed her. Why not? We were a fait accompli now. Besides, nobody could see much through all this fog anyway, if anybody was looking. "Maybe there isn't any Hell after all. I wonder how long I've loved you."

"Not long enough." She smiled all the way into my eyes. "So one night with me canceled out Hell for you? Or have you finally just had enough of your bad imagination?"

"She wasn't my imagination."

"I know."

"She was real. You know that, and so do a couple hundred people from last night." I considered. "All of whom are probably still talking about it. Maybe we should call in sick today."

"I didn't say she wasn't real. I'm saying she had to come from somewhere other than the usual place. *My* guess is that the somewhere is your pointy head."

"More like my pointy soul," I said darkly, turning away to brood over the deck rail.

She came up behind me and kissed my shoulder. "I'll take all the points off. Just give me time. In the meantime, if you have to repress something, repress Botticelli cherubs or cute little fuzzy bunny rabbits. Whatever won't hurt anybody if it gets out. Unlike the witch."

"She was *real*, Cass."

"I know. But so am I."

That struck me as being a perfectly wonderful fact. I was about to suggest that the sunrise start without us when the first light began to glow on the horizon. She held on tight. In five minutes, the sky was full of diffused gold, as the sun slowly began to burn off the fog. I felt as though we were two tiny figures in a light globe that God had just shaken.

"Beautiful, isn't it?" Cassie murmured.

"Very."

"I know it's trite—watching the sun come up together. But I don't care. I say we should dare to be trite. What do *you* say?"

I laughed. "Trite may be as close to normal as you and I ever get again." She didn't say anything. "Cass?"

"You're going to miss her, aren't you?" she asked softly.

She wasn't gone, not really. But I didn't see any point in telling Cassie so—not that morning, of all mornings. "Maybe. Some."

"Much?"

"I don't know," I lied.

"Well, I'll work on that too. It's not like I didn't know that you're a fixer-upper. But you have possibilities." She gave me an affectionate little squeeze. "Now, what if I call in sick for both of us, and we go back upstairs?"

"Works for me. Meet you there in a minute."

She took her time detaching herself but didn't argue and finally went in to find a phone. Not sure what I was feeling, I took my time collecting our coffee mugs.

Yes, I was going to miss Monica, but not for the reasons that Cassie probably thought. With Monica, I'd had an unbeatable excuse: She was a supernatural being, and she made me do it.

I had no such excuse now. Cassie was many things, but none of them supernatural, and although she may have started what eventually happened last night, I had willingly finished it. Somewhere in my pointy soul, a Big Stick God was bound to start pounding the drums soon, howling for blood.

Suddenly, though, I knew that was a crazy way to think. The world was full of consenting adults of greater, bolder wickedness—people who might whack a Big Stick God right back—who went on reveling in their pleasures, triumphantly alive. Cassie and I were alive, too. What was more, she was inside right now, guiltless, loving me, waiting.

To hell with what anyone else might think or say or do. I loved her, too, and we were going to work this thing through, one sunrise at a time.

Mugs in hand, I was almost to the door when a shadow fell over the deck, and a raven lighted on the deck rail. My heart stopped for a second—partly from dread and partly from hope.

"Monica?" I whispered.

The raven cocked its head. I stared at it, and it stared at me.

Then I remembered: Cassie was real, and Monica was—
Well, nevermore, if we were lucky.

I scared the bird away, locked the deck door behind me, and took the stairs up to the bedroom two at a time.

ABOUT THE AUTHOR

K. Simpson would sell her soul for rock & roll, but that's about it. She keeps an unholy mix of '80s music and Virgin Radio tracks on her iPods, and will neither confirm nor deny owning any ABBA.

Printed in the United States
147273LV00004B/25/P